SWEET VALLEY TWINS

Mary Is Missing

◇

Written by
Jamie Suzanne

Created by
FRANCINE PASCAL

A BANTAM SKYLARK BOOK®
NEW YORK • TORONTO • LONDON • SYDNEY • AUCKLAND

RL4, 008-012

MARY IS MISSING
A Bantam Skylark Book / February 1990

*Sweet Valley High® and Sweet Valley Twins are trademarks of
Francine Pascal*

Conceived by Francine Pascal

*Produced by Daniel Weiss Associates, Inc:
33 West 17th Street
New York, NY 10011*

Cover art by James Mathewuse

*Skylark Books is a registered trademark of Bantam Books, a division of
Bantam Doubleday Dell Publishing Group, Inc.*

ISBN 0-553-15778-7

Published simultaneously in the United States and Canada

---

*Bantam Books are published by Bantam Books, a division of Bantam
Doubleday Dell Publishing Group, Inc. Its trademark, consisting of
the words "Bantam Books" and the portrayal of a rooster, is Registered
in U.S. Patent and Trademark Office and in other countries. Marca
Registrada. Bantam Books, 666 Fifth Avenue, New York, New York 10103.*

PRINTED IN THE UNITED STATES OF AMERICA

OPM   0 9 8 7 6 5 4 3 2 1

A Mysterious Caller

"You took a telephone message two days ago and didn't tell us?" Jessica demanded. She sounded angry. "Who was it?"

"I don't know," Steven said vaguely. "I don't really remember. Some girl. She said to tell you something about money. She needed money and had to get away. Or she had money and needed to get away. Something like that."

The twins looked at each other. Elizabeth knew they were both asking themselves the same question. Could the call have been from Mary?

"Elizabeth," Jessica said, lowering her voice, "you don't suppose that Mary needed the Unicorn money for something, do you?" She sounded very worried. "Something like running away?"

Elizabeth shook her head. "If Mary was in that kind of trouble, she'd come to us," she said. "She wouldn't just take the money and go."

Jessica nodded. She knew Elizabeth was right. But that didn't help to answer the questions that weighed on Jessica's mind.

If it wasn't Mary who called, who was it?

And where was Mary?

Bantam Books in the SWEET VALLEY TWINS series
Ask your bookseller for the books you have missed

#1 BEST FRIENDS
#2 TEACHER'S PET
#3 THE HAUNTED HOUSE
#4 CHOOSING SIDES
#5 SNEAKING OUT
#6 THE NEW GIRL
#7 THREE'S A CROWD
#8 FIRST PLACE
#9 AGAINST THE RULES
#10 ONE OF THE GANG
#11 BURIED TREASURE
#12 KEEPING SECRETS
#13 STRETCHING THE TRUTH
#14 TUG OF WAR
#15 THE OLDER BOY
#16 SECOND BEST
#17 BOYS AGAINST GIRLS
#18 CENTER OF ATTENTION
#19 THE BULLY

#20 PLAYING HOOKY
#21 LEFT BEHIND
#22 OUT OF PLACE
#23 CLAIM TO FAME
#24 JUMPING TO CONCLUSIONS
#25 STANDING OUT
#26 TAKING CHARGE
#27 TEAMWORK
#28 APRIL FOOL!
#29 JESSICA AND THE BRAT ATTACK
#30 PRINCESS ELIZABETH
#31 JESSICA'S BAD IDEA
#32 JESSICA ON STAGE
#33 ELIZABETH'S NEW HERO
#34 JESSICA, THE ROCK STAR
#35 AMY'S PEN PAL
#36 MARY IS MISSING

Sweet Valley Twins Super Editions:
#1 THE CLASS TRIP
#2 HOLIDAY MISCHIEF
#3 THE BIG CAMP SECRET

Sweet Valley Twins Super Chiller
#1 THE CHRISTMAS GHOST

Mary Is Missing

One

◇

With a frown, Jessica Wakefield pushed a pile of clothes, record albums and magazines off her bed. She sat down and dialed Mary Wallace's number. Mary hadn't been at school for the past few days. Of course, that wasn't so bad. She could always make up her schoolwork. But it *was* too bad that she had missed Lila's after-school ice cream party the previous day. And worst of all, she had missed an important Unicorn meeting where she was supposed to give the treasurer's report. Jessica was worried. Mary would never have missed such an important meeting, unless she was *very* sick.

Jessica waited impatiently while the phone rang two, three, four times. Finally, just when she was ready to hang up, Mary's mother answered.

"Hello," Jessica said in her most polite voice. "This is Jessica Wakefield. I'd like to speak to Mary, please."

It took a moment for Mrs. Wallace to reply. "I'm sorry, Jessica," she finally said. She sounded a little bit sad. "Mary's not home."

Jessica was surprised. Not home? "She's not in the *hospital*, is she?" she blurted out.

"No, she isn't in the hospital," Mrs. Wallace sighed after a short pause.

Jessica waited, hoping Mrs. Wallace would tell her where Mary was and why she hadn't been at school. But when Mrs. Wallace didn't offer any explanation, Jessica went on.

"Can you tell me when she'll be back, or where I can reach her?" she asked. "I have to talk to her about something *really* important."

"I'm sorry, Jessica. I'm afraid Mary can't be reached," Mrs. Wallace replied curtly.

Jessica bit her lip. "Oh, OK. Well, please tell her I called," she said.

After Jessica hung up, she sat staring at the phone for a few minutes. Not only was she beginning to get worried, but she was curious, too. Where was Mary? And why was her mother acting so strange? Mrs. Wallace was usually very friendly. The whole thing seemed mysterious, Jessica thought. Very mysterious, indeed.

"Lizzie! Where are you?" Jessica yelled as she came charging onto the patio.

With a sigh, Elizabeth Wakefield put her finger in her book to mark her page. Her twin sister, Jessica, was calling her, and she knew her peace and quiet was about to end.

"Out here," Elizabeth called back. "At the thinking seat."

Jessica came toward her across the backyard, and pulled herself up onto the low branch where Elizabeth was already sitting. "Really, Lizzie," she said, tossing her long blond hair over her shoulder, "I don't know why you insist on hanging around under this old tree."

Elizabeth couldn't help smiling. For years, the huge pine tree had been their favorite place to read and talk and play. It was their own secret hideout. Now that she was older, Jessica didn't have any time to spend on the "thinking seat," as they called it. But the old tree was still one of Elizabeth's favorite spots, especially when she had a new Amanda Howard mystery to read.

On the outside, the Wakefield twins were identical. Both had long blond hair, blue-green eyes, and dimples in their left cheeks. It was almost impossible to tell them apart. But inside, they were very different. Jessica belonged to the Unicorn Club, an exclusive group of girls who thought they were as special and as beautiful as the mythical beast for which they were named. Every day the Unicorns tried to wear something purple—the color of royalty. Jessica was also a member of the Boosters, the middle school cheering squad that was mostly made up of Unicorn members. The Unicorns' favorite activities were talking about clothes and the most popular, best-looking boys, listening to rock music, and shopping at the Valley Mall. Jessica was impulsive, and a great schemer. But more often than not, her schemes backfired, and Elizabeth had to come to her rescue.

Elizabeth was as different from Jessica as she

could be. She cautiously thought everything through before deciding to do anything. The two girls sometimes joked that Elizabeth was more responsible because she was the older twin by four whole minutes, and Elizabeth frequently felt that those four minutes were more like four years. But whatever the reason, Elizabeth was certainly more serious than Jessica. At school, she was the editor of *The Sweet Valley Sixers*, the six-grade student newspaper. She also enjoyed writing and hoped to be a journalist some day. She had even gotten an electric typewriter on her last birthday, a gift that Jessica thought was extremely boring. Elizabeth loved to read as much as she loved to write, and mysteries and horse stories were her favorites.

Now she opened her book again, hoping Jessica would take the hint and let her get back to her story.

Jessica made a face. "Put your book down and listen, Lizzie," she commanded. "We've got a problem. A *big* problem."

Elizabeth sighed and closed the book again. Whenever Jessica wanted help solving a problem, it was always *their* problem.

"OK, Jess," she said. "What is it? What's the problem?"

"It's Mary."

Elizabeth looked at Jessica. For the most part, the twins chose very different friends, but Mary happened to be a friend they shared. Jessica and the other Unicorns thought Elizabeth's best friend, Amy Sutton, was a tomboy. Elizabeth thought most of Jessica's friends were snobs. And she thought Lila Fowler, Jessica's best friend, was the biggest snob of all. But Jessica knew that Elizabeth would be as concerned about Mary as she was, just as soon as she told her sister what was going on. "What's wrong with Mary?" Elizabeth asked. "Is she sick or something?"

Jessica threw up her hands. "That's just it," she said dramatically. "I don't know what's wrong with her! She hasn't been in school. I thought she was sick, so I called her house. But her mother said she wasn't home and wouldn't tell me where she is or when she's coming back either. I think Mary's missing."

Elizabeth frowned. She wished Jessica wasn't always so theatrical. "I know she hasn't been at school for a couple of days," she said patiently, "but I hardly think—"

"She missed Lila's ice cream party yesterday."

"Maybe she just didn't feel like eating ice cream," Elizabeth said. "Really, Jess, I don't see why—"

Jessica held up her hand. "And she missed the Unicorn meeting this afternoon," she said, with exaggerated emphasis.

"What a tragedy," Elizabeth remarked with a hint of sarcasm in her voice.

"It was a very *important* meeting," Jessica continued, ignoring her twin's comment. "We think we've got nearly fifty dollars in the treasury, enough for a big party. But we can't decide what to do until we know exactly how much money we've got. Mary's the only one who knows, and she was supposed to give us the treasurer's report today. She promised she would be there. She's never let us down!"

Elizabeth was beginning to understand Jessica's concern. Mary was reliable. You could always count on her to do what she said she was going to do. And Elizabeth knew that Mary took her job as the Unicorn's treasurer very seriously.

"She didn't let anybody know that she wasn't going to be at the meeting?" she asked.

Jessica shook her head. "Nobody's heard a

word from her in three days." She lowered her voice. "Lizzie, you don't think she might have run away, do you?"

Elizabeth knew that that was precisely what Jessica was thinking. A few days before, Mary had told them both—in the strictest confidence—that she and her mother had been arguing a lot lately, not about anything special, but about a lot of different things, big and small.

The twins fell silent, thinking about Mary. She had had a very eventful life just like a story in a book or a movie. When Mary was young, one of her mother's friends, Annie DeSalvo, kidnapped her. Annie had kept Mary for a long time, pretending she was her own daughter. And then one day, Annie disappeared. Mary was forced to live with several foster families after that, until she finally moved in with the Altmans, a couple who had no children of their own and lived down the street from the Wakefields. Mary loved the Altmans and was very happy with them, but she always believed that some day her real mother would find her. And Mary was right! Her mother searched for her for years before she finally found her. And then the two of them settled in Sweet Valley.

Recently, Mary's mother had remarried. The twins knew that Mary got along well with her stepfather, Tim. And he had been helping her resolve her differences with her mother. But he had gone to Santa Barbara for a few weeks to do some carpentry work on an old house that was being restored. Now Mary and her mother were alone together, and that meant an argument nearly every day.

"I don't think Mary would run away," Elizabeth said, considering Jessica's question seriously. "I know she's been having trouble with her mom lately, but that's because they're still getting used to each other after being separated for so long. I'm sure they'll work it out."

"But she's gone," Jessica argued. "And nobody knows where."

"Her mother must know," Elizabeth pointed out reasonably.

"If she knows, she's not telling." Jessica leaned closer to her sister. "In fact, she acted very strange on the phone. She sounded upset, and I have a feeling she didn't want me to know why."

Elizabeth sighed. "If you ask me, Jess, your imagination is working overtime again." She opened her book. "Now, if you don't mind, I'd like to finish this chapter," she said firmly. "This is an excellent mystery."

Jessica made a sour face at Elizabeth. "Sometimes I don't understand you, Lizzie. How can you sit there with your nose in a book when we've got a *real* mystery to solve?"

Elizabeth just smiled. For a second, Jessica stared at her twin, shaking her head. Then she turned and marched across the yard and into the house.

Amy Sutton was humming one of her favorite songs to herself as she walked down the street. She was on her way to Mary Wallace's house. Mary had promised to type an article that Amy had written for the next edition of *The Sweet Valley Sixers*, and Elizabeth needed it as soon as possible. Amy had been looking for Mary for two days to remind her that the article was due. But Mary was nowhere to be found. She hadn't been in the cafeteria at lunchtime, and Amy had overheard Jessica Wakefield and Lila Fowler saying that Mary had missed Lila's ice cream party the day before. The only explanation was that Mary was at home, sick with a cold or something. Amy thought it would be nice to visit Mary and see how she was feeling, and at the same time check up on her article.

As Amy turned the corner onto Mary's street, she saw Lila Fowler and Ellen Riteman coming toward her. Lila and Ellen were both members of the Unicorn Club. Amy wasn't particularly friendly with any of the Unicorns, except for Mary, and was one of the few nonmembers on the booster squad. Amy thought most of the Unicorns were stuck up and silly, but she tried not to be mean to them since she did have to go to booster practices with them. All they ever thought about was how pretty and how popular they were, without caring whether anybody outside their club *really* liked them. In fact, they had tried to keep Amy off the Boosters during tryouts earlier in the year. Their efforts had backfired when Amy turned out to be the best baton twirler in the sixth grade. She'd made the squad in spite of the Unicorns, and that was something for which Lila and Ellen would never forgive her.

"Hello, Amy," Lila said, as they approached. She tossed her light brown hair over her shoulder. "Are you going to Mary's house?" she demanded.

"Yes," Amy said, "as a matter of fact, I'm on my way there right now."

"Well, don't bother," Lila said, in a lofty, know-it-all voice.

"Why not?" Amy asked. "Mary is *my* friend, too." *Even if she is a Unicorn*, she added silently to herself.

Ellen lifted her nose. "You'd be wasting your time," she said, in a tone that matched Lila's, "Mary's not there."

"Not there?" Amy asked. "But I thought she was sick."

"So did we," Ellen said, with a glance at Lila. "So did everybody else, as a matter of fact. But it appears that she's not sick. She's just—not there, that's all. And her mother's not saying anything about where she might be."

Suddenly, Amy felt a little worried. *Where could Mary be?* she thought to herself. *And where is my* Sixers *article?*

At five-thirty, Elizabeth went inside and began to put plates on the table in the Wakefields' Spanish-style kitchen.

She was putting the forks out when her fourteen-year-old brother, Steven, came into the room and took two slices of bread out of the basket in the middle of the table. He had a faraway look in his eye, and Elizabeth couldn't help smiling. She knew what that meant: Steven was thinking about Laura, the pretty, brown-haired girl he had invited home for dinner a couple of days ago. Steven had become preoccupied and absentminded a lot recently.

Just then the telephone rang.

"I'll get it," Jessica called from upstairs. At the same instant, Steven shouted, "I'll get it," and went flying for the phone on the wall. Elizabeth's smile broadened. Every time Steven became interested in a new girl, there would always be a race to see whether he or Jessica would get to the phone first.

This time Jessica must have beaten him, because a few seconds later she called, "Mom, it's for you!"

Steven turned to Elizabeth. "Speaking of phones," he said, "I sort of remember that I was supposed to give you a message. Or maybe it was for Jess."

Elizabeth sighed. It was a strict family rule that they were supposed to write down all phone messages, but Steven usually forgot. And lately, with Laura always on his mind, he was even worse than usual.

Steven scratched his head. "Someone called a couple of days ago, I think. It was some girl."

"You took a telephone message two days ago and didn't tell us?" Jessica demanded, coming into the kitchen. She sounded angry. "Who was it?"

"I don't know," Steven said vaguely. "I don't really remember. Some girl. She said to tell you something about money. She needed money and had to get away. Or she had money and needed to get away. Something like that."

"Steven," Jessica wailed, "it sounds like a very important message. How could you have forgotten?"

Steven scowled. "Listen, you guys get tons of calls. How do you expect me to remember all of them?" He turned and started out of the room.

"That's why we're supposed to write them down," Elizabeth called after him as he walked away.

The twins looked at each other. Elizabeth knew they were both asking themselves the same question. Could the call have been from Mary?

"Elizabeth," Jessica said lowering her voice,

"you don't suppose that Mary needed the Unicorn money for something, do you?" She sounded very worried. "Something like running away?"

Elizabeth shook her head. "If Mary was in that kind of trouble, she'd come to us," she said. "She wouldn't just take the money and go."

Jessica nodded. She knew Elizabeth was right. It was dumb to think Mary might have taken the Unicorns' money, for any reason. Mary was much too honest to do something like that. But that didn't help to answer the questions that weighed on Jessica's mind.

If it wasn't Mary who called, who was it?

And *where* was Mary?

Two

◇

At school the next day, Jessica, Lila and Ellen were eating their lunches as they read the edition of *The Sweet Valley Sixers* which had been handed out that morning.

"I know it seems impossible," Ellen said, throwing down her paper, "but there isn't a *word* about your ice cream party in this whole newspaper. I've read every page twice, just to make sure." She frowned across the table at Jessica. "Why didn't Elizabeth put something in the paper about Lila's party, Jessica?"

"I—" was all Jessica could say before Lila interrupted her.

"And," Lila said, scowling over the top of her copy, "there's not even an article about the letter I got from the Donny Diamond Fan Club. I told Elizabeth all about that letter! I even showed it to her. It had Donny Diamond's signature stamped on it. I thought 'LILA FOWLER RECEIVES LETTER FROM DONNY DIAMOND' would have made a terrific headline." She gave Jessica a stern look. "You know, I think the *Sixers* staff is leaving the Unicorns out of the newspaper on purpose."

Ellen nodded. "I agree. Remember the party I had a couple of weeks ago in honor of Johnny Buck's birthday? The *Sixers* didn't cover that either, and it was one of the biggest social events of the year. The only explanation is that we're being deliberately discriminated against."

Lila and Ellen both turned to Jessica with angry looks on their faces.

"Well, don't blame me," Jessica said. She folded her paper and stuck it into her notebook. "I don't have anything to do with the *Sixers*. Elizabeth is the one who decides what to print.

That is, Elizabeth and the other newspaper staff members."

"That's exactly the problem!" Lila exclaimed. "Elizabeth and her friends have complete control over what goes into *our* class newspaper. And since Elizabeth doesn't like the Unicorns—" She shrugged elaborately. "It's not exactly surprising that the Unicorns never make the paper."

"That's right, Lila!" Ellen cried. "The only time we get a mention in the *Sixers* is when we sponsor some kind of fund-raising event. It's almost as if the Unicorns don't exist!"

"It's not my fault," Jessica wailed. "I tell Elizabeth absolutely everything the Unicorns do. Well, almost everything," she added hastily, remembering that there were some important Unicorn secrets that nobody outside the club was supposed to know about. Jessica turned to Ellen. "I told Elizabeth all about your weekend in Santa Monica, *and* I told her about the cute boy we talked to at the mall. I can't help it if there's not a word about any of it in the newspaper."

"I'm not surprised," Ellen said. "Because it's a plot. A plot against the Unicorns."

"Well," Jessica replied, exasperated. "If it's a plot, what exactly do you want to do about it?"

That, she thought to herself, *should keep them quiet for a while*.

"I think, Jessica," Lila announced, "that you'd better talk to Elizabeth about this immediately. Tell her we're very upset about the way she's ignoring the Unicorns."

"But—" Jessica began.

"Don't tell her we think it's a plot," Lila went on. "Not right away, anyway. First we'll give her a chance to be fair."

"Uh, OK," Jessica said reluctantly. "I'll talk to her." Jessica decided that it was time to change the subject. She looked around the crowded lunchroom. "Have either of you seen Mary Wallace today?"

"No," Lila said, "I haven't. And I've been looking for her for days. Ellen and I even went over to her house yesterday afternoon, but her mother said she wasn't there. It really bugs me that she disappeared just when we needed her treasurer's report. I'm getting annoyed with her, aren't you?"

Jessica sighed. "I guess," she agreed. But Jessica was more *worried* about Mary's disappearance than she was annoyed. "Do you guys think

I should go over to her house and see what I can find out?"

Jessica felt sure that if she went to Mary's, she would spot some clue about where she was. Maybe Mary was sick after all, and for some reason her mother didn't want people to know. Or maybe she *had* run away, but had left behind some kind of clue about where she was going.

"That's a very good idea, Jessica," Lila said approvingly. "Do you think Mrs. Wallace would let you into Mary's room?"

"Well," Jessica said. "I'd have to think of a good reason, but I think she would. Why, what do you have in mind?"

"You should try to get into her room," Ellen answered helpfully, "and then search for the Unicorns' treasury."

"Yes, that's the perfect plan!" Lila said in a decisive tone. "Go right after school. And call me the minute you get home," she added, "so you can tell me what you find."

Jessica nodded. "OK," she said.

Jessica had the feeling that Lila and Ellen were more interested in the treasury than they were in Mary. And in a way she could understand their point of view. Ever since Steven had given her the confused message the night before, Jessica had been very worried about Mary. And, even though she knew it was silly, she was still a tiny bit worried about the Unicorn money. Jessica didn't think it would hurt to see what she could find out in Mary's room, even though Elizabeth would definitely have said it was wrong to snoop through Mary's private things—and wrong to doubt their friend.

When school was over that afternoon, Jessica went straight to the Wallaces'.

Mrs. Wallace looked slightly startled when she answered the door. "Why, hello, Jessica," she said. "I . . . I wasn't expecting you."

"I stopped by to pick up a library book that Mary borrowed from me," Jessica said. "It's due on Monday, and I'll be in trouble if I don't take it back." It was true. Mary *had* borrowed the book, and it *was* due on Monday. "I wonder if I could go up to Mary's room and get it."

Mrs. Wallace hesitated for a moment. "Well, I guess so," she said reluctantly, opening the door and letting Jessica in. "Do you think you can find it?"

"Oh, I'm sure I can," Jessica said eagerly,

heading for the stairs before Mrs. Wallace could change her mind. "It's probably on her desk."

Jessica dashed up the stairs and into Mary's room. *It looks fairly normal*, Jessica thought. There was a pile of books on the desk, and Jessica's library book was there, just as she'd expected. Mary's math homework was on the desk, too, as if she'd been interrupted in the middle of it.

Quickly, Jessica went over to the desk and opened the top drawer. She knew that was where Mary kept her important things, and that was where she thought the Unicorn treasury would be. But much to her disappointment, the money wasn't there. She found only old photographs and letters.

Then Jessica looked around the room carefully. Something didn't seem quite normal. It took a second before she realized what it was. Mary was usually a very neat person. But the closet door and several dresser drawers were open. Clothes were pulled out, and some of them were tossed onto the bed, as if Mary had been sorting through them in a hurry.

Jessica narrowed her eyes. She hated to admit it, but the homework on the desk, the clothes, the mess—seemed to indicate that Mary had run away. And then she saw something else, something that really surprised her. It was Max, Mary's teddy bear. The worn and tattered stuffed animal was sitting in his usual spot on Mary's pillow.

If it were anybody but Mary, Jessica would probably have laughed at the idea of a seventh-grader sleeping with a teddy bear every night, even when she went to stay overnight with friends. But Jessica understood why Mary needed the comfort of her dear old friend Max. Loving, faithful Max had been with her for all those years Mary was separated from her mother, and he was with her still.

That was what surprised Jessica. It looked very much as if Mary had run away—but why hadn't she taken Max with her?

That question was still bothering Jessica an hour later, as she sat on the floor in her room, listening to records and trying to decide what she should do. Lila was expecting her to call and tell her what she had found out. And there was so much she *could* tell Lila; about Mary's messy room, the unfinished homework, and Max. But when she thought about it, Jessica realized that she couldn't tell Lila anything. She had promised Mary that she would never tell anyone about her problems with her mother. If she told Lila what she'd seen, Lila would probably come to the conclusion that Mary had run away.

Jessica was so deep in thought that she jumped when the telephone rang. She got up and walked into the hall to answer it.

"Hello?" she said absently.

"Well," Lila demanded eagerly, "what did you find out?"

Jessica hesitated. "Not much," she replied at last.

"Did you get into Mary's room?"

"Yes, but there wasn't much to see," Jessica answered. "Just some clothes and books and her teddy bear." It was the truth, Jessica told herself—it just wasn't the *whole* truth.

Lila sighed. "You didn't find the Unicorn treasury?"

"No, I didn't."

"Now I'm sure," Lila said firmly, "that something weird is going on. It's very strange that Mary disappeared just when she was supposed to give a report on the money in our treasury."

Jessica took a deep breath. "Lila, what do you mean by that?" she asked.

"Nothing," Lila replied. "All I know is that we'd better find that money. Every penny of it."

"Oh, don't worry," Jessica said breezily, with a little laugh. "As soon as we find Mary, she'll give us the treasurer's report *and* the money. It's silly to suspect—"

"I didn't say I suspected anything," Lila cut in. "You're jumping to conclusions." There was a pause, and then Lila said, "Jessica, are you sure you've told us everything you know about Mary? I mean, you don't know something that you're not telling us, do you?"

"Know something?" Jessica said innocently. "What in the world could I possibly know?"

Lila wasn't convinced. "Jessica, if you know anything about Mary that would help us, you'd *better* tell. Don't forget your Unicorn oath. You're supposed to be loyal to the Unicorns."

For a moment, Jessica felt guilty. Yes, she was a Unicorn, and she was loyal. But Mary was a Unicorn, too. She had to be loyal to Mary, just as much as to the other Unicorns. Anyway, she knew there was an explanation for Mary's absence, a good explanation. All she had to do was find it. For that she would need more time. And to get more time, she would have to convince Lila that everything was just fine.

Jessica did her best to imitate the tone Elizabeth used when she thought Jessica was exaggerating. "Don't be silly, Lila," she said. "You're making this little thing sound like a huge mystery. And it isn't a mystery at all. We'll find Mary before you know it, and there will be a good explanation for everything."

Lila sighed. "I hope so, Jess," she said. But she still didn't sound completely convinced.

After she said goodbye to Lila, Jessica put down the phone and sat thinking for a few minutes. Then she got up and went to find Elizabeth.

Elizabeth stopped writing and looked up from her history homework when Jessica came into her room. By the time Jessica had finishing telling her what she had seen at Mary's that day, Elizabeth looked upset.

"Mary's teddy bear was on her bed?" she asked. "Are you sure?"

"Of course I'm sure," Jessica replied. "And not only that, but there were clothes all over the place. Her room was really messy."

"Wow. That's not like Mary at all," Elizabeth said, chewing on the end of her pencil. "She's usually so neat. She always hangs everything up."

"I know." Jessica sighed. "What do you think, Lizzie?"

"I don't know what to think," she confessed. "It sounds like a mystery."

"A real mystery," Jessica agreed.

Three

◇

"Do you like this, Elizabeth?" Jessica asked, holding up a long, purple, beaded necklace. It was Saturday, and the twins were shopping at the Valley Mall.

Elizabeth looked at the necklace. It wasn't the sort of thing she would buy. But she just nodded and said, "It looks like a Unicorn necklace."

"That's what I think, too," Jessica said. "I'm going to get it."

The twins had spent the morning doing what Jessica loved best, shopping. But Elizabeth noticed that Jessica didn't seem to be having a very good time. That could only mean one thing—she was still worrying about Mary.

Around noon, the twins had hamburgers and chocolate milkshakes. After they finished eating, they walked around, looking in store windows. Then Elizabeth suggested that they go to the movies. Jessica brightened up at once.

"Hey, that's a great idea," she exclaimed. "I want to see the new Brent Baines movie. Janet Howell says it's terrific. And it's a mystery—your favorite!" Jessica teased her twin.

"Great," Elizabeth agreed enthusiastically. "I wonder when the next show starts."

"Hmmm. Let's go buy a newspaper," Jessica said.

Elizabeth looked around. "Hey, Jess." She pointed to a folded-up paper lying on a nearby bench. "There's a paper!"

"Wow, what luck," Jessica said, picking up the newspaper and removing the movie section. The girls sat down on the bench.

While Jessica was looking for the movie time, Elizabeth picked up the other section of the paper and glanced at it. "That's funny," she said.

"What?" Jessica asked absently, running her finger down the movie listings.

"There are holes in this paper. Somebody's been clipping little pieces out of it."

Jessica shrugged. "So what? Somebody clipped out an article, that's all. Or maybe a picture. People cut up newspapers all the time."

"But words have been clipped out," Elizabeth said. She showed Jessica one of the pages. "See? The first word in this headline is missing. Isn't that weird?"

"Well, at least the movie page is all here," Jessica said with satisfaction. "That's all we care about."

"I know. But who would go to the trouble of cutting out all these words?" Elizabeth wondered out loud. "And why?" She started to look through the newspaper again. If one of Amanda Howard's heroines had found something like this, it would probably be a clue to a mystery. She would probably sit right down and figure out which words were missing. The missing word in the headline, for instance. That word had to be "police," Elizabeth decided, because the headline read "—ARREST MAN FOR JAY-WALKING."

"Terrific!" Jessica suddenly exclaimed. She threw the movie section into the trash can beside the bench. "The movie's starting in ten minutes. Come on, Lizzie, quit fooling around with that paper and let's go!"

"OK," Elizabeth said. She started to throw the rest of the paper away. But then, on an impulse, she folded it up and tucked it into her backpack. It might be kind of fun to figure out the missing words, she thought.

"That was great!" Jessica exclaimed, as the twins walked out of the theater a couple of hours later. She sighed. "I just *love* Brent Baines. He's *so* cute! Don't you think, Elizabeth?"

Before Elizabeth could answer, Lila Fowler and Ellen Riteman walked up to them.

"Hello," Lila said.

"Hi, Jess. Hi, Elizabeth," Ellen said, but Elizabeth didn't think she looked too friendly.

"Hi," Jessica said. Elizabeth gave her a quick glance. Her twin didn't look too happy about bumping into Lila and Ellen, and that was unusual.

"Have you heard from Mary yet?" Lila asked.

Jessica bit her lip. "Not yet," she said. And then she changed the subject. "Are you on your way to see this movie? Brent Baines is so great."

"I'm surprised you didn't want to go to the movies with us, Jessica," Lila said. "You knew we were going today. You're not avoiding us, are you?"

"Why would I do that?" Jessica asked. Elizabeth noticed that she sounded a little guilty.

"Maybe because you know something about where Mary is, and you don't want to tell us," Ellen said.

"That is, maybe you know where Mary went with the Unicorn treasury," Lila added.

Elizabeth frowned. "Hey," she said, "you're not suggesting that Mary took that money, are you?"

Lila gave her an icy smile. "Actually, Elizabeth, we're discussing Unicorn business."

"That's right," Ellen chimed in. "And you're not a Unicorn."

Elizabeth nodded. Ellen was right, she wasn't a Unicorn. Of course, she'd been invited to join at the same time that Jessica had. But when she'd turned the invitation down, Lila and Ellen probably held it against her.

"That's not important," Jessica said. "What's

important is that we find Mary, so she can clear all this up."

Lila nodded. "That's right, Jessica," she said loftily. "That's exactly what we keep telling you. We have to find Mary so she can clear all this up."

Ellen leaned forward, watching Jessica intently. "You know, Jessica, this is important Unicorn business," she said. "If you know something about Mary and the treasury and you're hiding it, you're as guilty as Mary is."

Jessica squirmed. "Oh, don't be silly," she scoffed. She was smiling, but Elizabeth thought she looked nervous. After all, she *was* hiding something. Elizabeth knew Jessica hadn't mentioned anything to Lila and Ellen about Mary's problems with her mother or about what she saw at Mary's house. Elizabeth was proud of Jessica for keeping her promise to Mary. "Besides," Jessica added. "Who said that Mary is *guilty* of anything?"

After a minute or two, Lila and Ellen said goodbye and went into the movie. Jessica turned to Elizabeth with an uneasy laugh.

"Lila and Ellen don't really think Mary took the money," she said. "Everybody knows how serious and responsible Mary is about money. That's why the Unicorns elected her treasurer."

But Elizabeth didn't feel reassured. What Lila and Ellen thought seemed clear to her—they thought Mary was a thief. It made her angry that anyone would think such a thing about her friend. She was sure Mary hadn't done anything wrong, but no matter how hard she tried, she couldn't come up with a good explanation for Mary's disappearance.

Later that afternoon, Elizabeth remembered the newspaper she'd put into her book bag. She got it out and laid it down in front of her on her desk. She could figure out some of the clipped-out words quickly. But some of the others seemed impossible. Elizabeth concentrated on the paper for a long time, and suddenly she had a brilliant idea. She checked the date on the newspaper and then went downstairs to the den, where she found the Sweet Valley newspaper from the day before on the coffee table. She grabbed the paper, ran upstairs again, laid the two papers side by side and began to compare them. On page one, the word "safe" had been clipped out, and the word "call." Down at the bottom of the page, "will be" was gone, and on the third page, "your."

Curious, Elizabeth reached for a pad of paper and began to write down the missing words. When she'd finished, there were twelve words on the list:

SAFE
CALL
WILL BE
YOUR
POLICE
DAUGHTER
SOON
IN
DON'T
IS
TOUCH

Elizabeth leaned forward eagerly. She loved word games and was very good at them.

"Let's see," she said to herself. "How can I make a sentence out of these words?"

After several tries, Elizabeth sat back in her chair and stared at the message she had printed in big letters across her yellow pad: YOUR DAUGHTER IS SAFE WILL BE IN TOUCH SOON DON'T CALL POLICE. Her heart was beating fast, and she was almost breathless with astonishment.

Just then Jessica burst into Elizabeth's room. "Liz, we need to talk," she began in a rush, "I just called Mrs. Wallace to check on Mary, and she—"

Elizabeth turned around. "Come here, Jess," she said.

Surprised by the tone in her sister's voice, Jessica went over to the desk, where Elizabeth was sitting.

"Look," Elizabeth said, pointing at the pad.

Jessica sighed. "I'll look at it later, Elizabeth. I have something important to tell you! Mrs. Wallace was almost rude to me on the phone just now."

"Rude?" Elizabeth asked, surprised.

"Yes. She said she wasn't sure when Mary would be back. And then she told me not to call again. Can you believe it?"

Elizabeth shook her head. "That's not like Mrs. Wallace at all," she said slowly.

"No, it isn't," Jessica agreed. "I think something's wrong. I can't imagine why Mrs. Wallace wouldn't tell us where Mary is."

Again, Elizabeth pointed at the pad of paper. "Maybe I know why. Remember that newspaper we found this afternoon? I've figured out which words are missing. If you make a sentence out of them, this is what they say."

Jessica bent over to read. "Your daughter is safe . . . will be in touch soon . . . don't call police." She gasped. "Liz! It sounds like—like a kidnapper's note!"

"That's *exactly* what it sounds like," Elizabeth said grimly.

Jessica looked back at the paper. When she spoke, her voice was a whisper.

"The only person we know who is missing," she said faintly, "is Mary." She looked up at her twin, her eyes wide. "Lizzie, do you think Mary has been kidnapped?"

Four

◇

Elizabeth shook her head. "I don't know what to think," she said slowly, looking down at the pad of paper. "The words don't make sense any other way—at least, not that I can see. But it's awfully hard to believe that we could just stumble over a kidnapper's note. I mean, it's like something out of an Amanda Howard mystery. Things like this just don't happen in real life!"

"Yes, they do!" Jessica exclaimed. "Now it all makes sense. Somebody kidnapped Mary and sent her mother this note. That's why Mrs. Wallace is so upset. I bet she's afraid that if she talks to anyone, she'll put Mary's life in danger. It's the only logical explanation, Elizabeth!"

Elizabeth had learned the hard way to be suspicious of Jessica's logical explanations. And in this case, Jessica's explanation was pretty farfetched. Elizabeth was a logical, down-to-earth person, and to her it seemed unbelievable that the two of them would stumble onto something as big as this.

But she had to agree that the facts appeared to support Jessica's explanation. First, Mary was missing. Second, her mother was terribly upset about something. And there was the note, on the desk right in front of them: YOUR DAUGHTER IS SAFE WILL BE IN TOUCH SOON DON'T CALL POLICE.

"I think," Elizabeth said slowly, "that we ought to call the police and tell them about this."

Jessica shook her head. "No, Lizzie," she said forcefully. "That's exactly what the kidnapper says *not* to do. If the police start looking for Mary, the kidnapper will think Mrs. Wallace got in touch with them. Then there's no telling what might happen to Mary."

"But we can't handle this all by ourselves!" Elizabeth exclaimed. "I mean, if Mary really has been kidnapped, her life is in danger!"

At that instant, the doorbell rang downstairs. The twins heard Amy Sutton's voice, and a moment later, her footsteps on the stairs.

"Hi, Elizabeth," Amy said cheerfully, coming into the room. "Hi, Jessica." She sat down on Elizabeth's bed. "Elizabeth, I have a problem."

Elizabeth bit her lip. "*You've* got a problem?" she asked, glancing at the note.

"Yeah. It's about Mary Wallace."

"Mary?" Elizabeth and Jessica repeated at the same time.

Amy glanced from one twin to the other, looking a little puzzled. "Yes, Mary. Listen, the other day—"

Jessica leaned forward. "Do you know where she is?"

"Have you heard from her?" Elizabeth asked eagerly.

"No," Amy replied, "I haven't heard from her. *That's* my problem."

"Oh." Jessica sighed. Elizabeth shook her head.

Amy frowned at the twins, and then continued. "Remember the interview with Coach Cassels that I'm writing for the *Sixers*?" Amy asked Elizabeth.

Elizabeth nodded. "What about it? Is it finished?"

"Yes, it's finished," Amy replied. "But my mom's typewriter is broken, and I gave the article to Mary to type. Now I can't find Mary anywhere. She's disappeared into thin air!"

Elizabeth and Jessica exchanged looks.

"Hey, what's going on?" Amy asked, sensing that something was disturbing the twins. "You guys look upset. Is everything OK?"

Elizabeth looked at Jessica and raised her eyebrows. Jessica nodded. "Tell her," Jessica said.

Elizabeth picked up the pad and handed it to Amy. "What would you say about this?" she asked.

Amy read the words out loud. "Your daughter is safe . . . will be in touch soon . . . don't call police." She looked up at the twins, grinning. "All right," she said, "what's up? Who have you kidnapped? Mary Wallace?" She looked around the room. "I'll bet you've got her in the closet, huh?"

"It's not a joke, Amy," Jessica said soberly.

"Jessica's right," Elizabeth said. "This is for real." She told Amy about the newspaper and about what Jessica had seen in Mary's room.

"*And* Mrs. Wallace is acting really weird," Jessica added. "She won't tell anyone where Mary is or when she'll be back."

Amy frowned. "You know," she said slowly, "there's something else, too. I saw Mrs. Wallace at the bank yesterday."

"At the bank?" Elizabeth asked.

"Yes. I was there with my mom, and Mrs. Wallace was standing in the next line. I noticed that she looked awfully worried. Maybe she was taking out money to pay the ransom."

"For the kidnapper's ransom, of course!" Jessica agreed.

"I think you're both jumping to conclusions," Elizabeth said.

"But it makes sense," Jessica insisted. "Don't you see? The kidnapper took Mary, then sent the note to her mother. And now Mrs. Wallace has to pay a ransom to get Mary back." She shook her head. "All of that is really obvious. My only question is, who would want to kidnap Mary?"

Suddenly Amy snapped her fingers. "I know!" she exclaimed. "I know who would want to do it!"

"You do?" Elizabeth and Jessica asked in unison.

"Of course!" Amy declared. "Annie DeSalvo!"

Elizabeth gave her a doubtful look. "Annie DeSalvo? Isn't she—"

"The woman who kidnapped Mary before!" Jessica exclaimed, finishing Elizabeth's sentence. "When Mary was a little girl! Why didn't I think of that?"

"That's right," Amy said.

"Makes sense to me," Jessica said with a nod.

Elizabeth wasn't convinced. "Do you actually think," she asked slowly, "that Annie DeSalvo kidnapped Mary *again*? Why would she do that?"

"Maybe she's mad at Mary's mom," Amy offered. "Maybe she found out that Mrs. Wallace and Mary are together again and she's angry about it."

"Or maybe she misses Mary," Jessica suggested, "and wants her back."

"Or maybe she thinks this is an easy way to make some money," Amy added. "I can think of lots of reasons."

"That's right," Jessica said. "But the facts all point to one thing. Mary's been kidnapped, and Annie DeSalvo did it!"

Elizabeth stood up. "In that case," she said, "we have to call the police."

"But we can't!" Jessica wailed. "That could put Mary's life in danger!"

"I'm with Elizabeth," Amy said. "Annie DeSalvo

probably won't hurt Mary. I think it's safe to tell the police."

"But we don't know for sure that the kidnapper is Annie DeSalvo," Jessica objected. "We're only guessing. And anyway, even if it *is* Annie DeSalvo, she could run away with Mary again anytime. If she thinks Mrs. Wallace called the police she might take Mary someplace nobody would ever find her."

Elizabeth was trying to think of a compromise. "Maybe we could call Officer Carey," she said finally. "We could just tell him Mary's been missing for a couple of days and we're worried that something's happened to her."

Jessica looked half convinced. She knew Officer Carey. He had recently helped the twins find a stolen scrapbook that belonged to Mrs. Harrington, an actress friend of theirs.

"I think that's a good idea," Amy said. "We don't have to tell him about the note or who we suspect."

"Well, all right," Jessica said reluctantly.

A few minutes later, Elizabeth hung up the telephone. "Officer Carey said he would look into the situation himself," she told Jessica and

Amy with a smile. "And he said it was wonderful that we were so concerned about a friend. He'll call back when he's got something to tell us."

Amy glanced at her watch. "Well, I can stay for another hour," she said. "I hope he'll call back before then."

"Me, too," Elizabeth said. "We could go swimming while we're waiting."

"That's a great idea," Amy said. "But I'll have to borrow a suit from you."

The girls changed into their suits and went out to the backyard.

Amy and Elizabeth splashed around in the Wakefields' pool while Jessica sat on the patio looking through a fashion magazine. A little while later, Steven came out and called Elizabeth to the phone.

Elizabeth dashed inside, and the other girls followed. It was Officer Carey.

"I just wanted to tell you," he said, "that I talked with Mary Wallace's mother personally, just a few minutes ago. She assured me that everything is fine. Mary has gone away with some friends. Mrs. Wallace expects her daughter back sometime very soon." He paused. "So it doesn't look like we have a missing-person case, Elizabeth. Just a case of a girl taking a trip."

Elizabeth inhaled deeply. "OK, Officer Carey," she said. "Thanks for checking." She put down the phone and turned to the others.

"Mary's mom told him that everything is just fine," she said slowly. "She said that Mary's on a trip, and she'll be home soon."

"So we're right back where we started," Jessica moaned.

"No, we're not," Elizabeth replied. "I trust Officer Carey. If he thought something was wrong, he would've told us."

"But he wouldn't find out if something's wrong just by checking with Mary's mother," Jessica pointed out. "She isn't going to tell him anything. She's following the kidnapper's instructions. Anyway, what about the note?"

Elizabeth frowned. "There could be other explanations for the note," she said. "Maybe it's part of a game that somebody's playing, like a scavenger hunt, or something like that."

"If it's a game, it's the weirdest game ever," Jessica complained. "And what about the money Mrs. Wallace took out of the bank?"

Elizabeth folded her arms over her chest. "Well,

we don't know how much money it was, or whether it had anything to do with Mary," she reminded her twin. "I vote we drop the whole thing."

"I guess I agree with Elizabeth," Amy said reluctantly. "I mean, we don't have any real evidence."

"That's right," Elizabeth said. "Mary will probably be back at school on Monday."

"Well, I don't think she will be," Jessica said firmly. "I think there's something weird about the way Mrs. Wallace is acting. I think the note is a ransom note, and that Annie DeSalvo wrote it. Besides, if Mary knew she was going away she would have let us know she'd be missing the Unicorn meeting. And she probably would have called Amy, too, about her article."

"Well, let's just wait for now," Elizabeth replied reasonably. "If Mary's not back at school soon, we'll think of something to do."

"Yeah," Amy agreed. "We'll think of something."

Five

By Sunday morning, things seemed much clearer to Jessica. If Elizabeth and Amy would not accept her explanation of Mary's disappearance, she was going to find somebody who would. She decided to start with Lila Fowler and Ellen Riteman. After all, they were very concerned about Mary's absence. And if they knew that Mary had been kidnapped, they would stop thinking that she might have run away with the Unicorns' money.

Jessica smiled as she knocked on Lila's front door. She was positive that as soon as Lila and

Ellen heard her explanation of Mary's disappearance, they would be impressed. They would probably tell her what a brilliant and logical mind she had.

But she was wrong. Lila and Ellen weren't at all impressed.

"I don't believe it," Ellen said firmly, after Jessica had finished her story. "Do you, Lila?"

"Not a word of it," Lila said. "In fact, I think you're inventing it, Jessica. To cover up something."

"To cover up what?" Jessica asked.

Ellen frowned. "That's what we're not sure about. Maybe it's got to do with the money. Maybe not. But whatever it is, it's obvious you've been hiding something from us."

Jessica pressed her lips together. She couldn't tell them about Mary and her mother. She'd promised. She straightened her shoulders. "I can prove what I'm saying," she said. "I can prove that Mary's been kidnapped."

"Prove it?" Lila asked skeptically. "How?"

Jessica looked over her shoulder to make sure nobody was listening. "We'll stake out the Wallaces' house," she said, lowering her voice. "If there's something strange going on, we'll find out what it is."

"Stake out their house?" Lila asked doubtfully.

"You know, the way detectives do on television," Jessica said. "There's a vacant lot next door to Mary's. If we hide there, we'll be able to see whoever comes and goes. We'll even be able to see into the Wallaces' living room. And if Mrs. Wallace has her windows open and anybody calls on the phone, we'll be able to—"

"That won't work," Ellen objected. "Besides, it'll be boring. I think we should ride our bikes to the beach."

Lila held up her hand. "Wait a minute, Ellen. What were you saying, Jessica?"

"I was saying that we'll probably be able to hear the conversation if anybody calls Mrs. Wallace."

"So if Mary calls her mother, we might be able to figure out where she is," Lila said, considering the plan.

"The kidnapper might call, but Mary's not going to," Jessica said. "I'm sure the kidnapper won't let—"

"Forget that silly kidnapping story," Lila said impatiently. "If we stake out Mary's house, we might be able to find out where she's gone. And where our money is. Come on. We're going to the Wallaces."

"I told you it would be boring," Ellen said after they'd spent an hour watching the Wallaces' house. "We should have gone to the beach."

Lila sighed. "I'm beginning to think you're right, Ellen," she said. She scratched her ankle. "I'm getting bitten by ants or something."

Jessica pushed a branch out of her hair and shifted uncomfortably. She was getting tired of sitting in one position and listening to Ellen complain. She was getting bored, too. In detective movies, stakeouts always seemed a lot more exciting than this. Something always happened, and usually in the first few minutes. But still, Jessica was determined to stay, and to make sure that Lila and Ellen stayed, too. It was the only way she could think of to convince them that her story was true.

"I think it's time to quit," Ellen said. "I'm hot and thirsty. Let's go get something to drink."

But at that minute, the telephone rang in the Wallaces' house, and the girls fell silent and listened. Mrs. Wallace picked it up on the second ring, as if she'd been waiting for someone to call.

"Hello," she said. And then, "Yes, of course. I was just getting ready to leave." A pause. And then, almost impatiently, "No, of course I won't be late. And I'll bring what I promised—all of it. None of it's marked, of course. It's all small stuff." Another pause. "Yes, I understand. But it'll take me longer to get the rest of it together." A moment later, she said goodbye and hung up.

"What do you suppose—" Ellen began, but Jessica broke in anxiously.

"She was talking to the kidnapper!" she exclaimed. "She's going to pay the ransom!"

"What makes you so sure?" Lila demanded.

"She said none of it was marked," Jessica said, feeling important. "Don't you ever watch television? Kidnappers always ask for the ransom to be paid in unmarked bills. And I happen to know that Mrs. Wallace went to the bank on Friday. I'll bet she was taking out money to pay the kidnapper."

Lila looked at her. "How do you know she went to the bank?"

Jessica smiled slyly, "I have my sources," she said.

Lila looked back at the house. "I wonder where she's going. And who she's going to meet."

"She's going to meet the kidnapper!" Jessica said dramatically. A minute later, when Mary's mother came out of the house, Jessica was even more sure. Mrs. Wallace was carrying a suitcase, a bundle of clothes that Jessica recognized as Mary's, and Max, Mary's teddy bear.

Ellen squinted. "A suitcase?" she asked in a hoarse whisper, as Mrs. Wallace got into her car. "What's she taking that suitcase for? And isn't that Mary's teddy bear?"

"Don't you know anything?" Jessica asked scornfully. "People always put ransom money into a suitcase. They have to carry it in something because the kidnapper wants the money in lots of small bills instead of a few large ones. Didn't you hear her say she was bringing all small stuff? And look—she's got clothes for Mary, and Mary's favorite teddy bear! You guys know Mary always sleeps with that bear."

Lila looked impressed. "I admit it, Jessica," she said reluctantly, "you seem to be right."

"I know I'm right," Jessica said. She stood up

as Mrs. Wallace's car backed out of the drive. "Come on. We can't let her get away!"

"Come on?" Ellen asked fretfully. "Where are we going?"

"We're going to follow her, of course," Jessica said. "Let's get our bikes! Hurry!"

The girls pedaled fast enough to keep Mrs. Wallace's car in sight for a couple of blocks, but then they lost her in traffic. An hour later, when they returned to the Wallace house after stopping at the Dairi Burger for chocolate shakes, they saw Mrs. Wallace pulling into the driveway. When she got out, she wasn't carrying the suitcase or the teddy bear.

"What did I tell you?" Jessica demanded. "She paid off the kidnapper!"

"But," Lila said slowly, "where's Mary?"

"Yeah, if Mrs. Wallace paid the ransom," Ellen said, "wouldn't the kidnappers have let Mary go?"

"Not yet," Jessica said firmly. "Didn't you hear Mrs. Wallace? This was only the first payment. The kidnapper demanded more money. Mrs. Wallace said that it would take her a while to get the rest of it together."

Lila nodded. "You're right, Jessica," she said

admiringly. "You were pretty smart to figure all this out."

Jessica just smiled.

Even though it was a beautiful Sunday afternoon, Elizabeth and Amy had decided to go to the library. All of the social studies classes at Sweet Valley Middle School were studying Mexico, and the girls wanted to do some research for a report they were going to give together. Because it was such a pretty day, the reference section at the library was almost deserted and unusually quiet. It was so quiet that Elizabeth could hear the rustling of paper at a desk all the way on the other side of the card catalog. Then Elizabeth heard something else. Someone at the other end of the aisle was ripping something! Elizabeth could feel anger boiling up inside her. Somebody was tearing up a book! For Elizabeth, who felt very passionate about books, destroying one—especially one that belonged to the library—was a horrible thing to do.

Amy looked up from the notes she had been making. "What's wrong, Elizabeth?" she whispered.

Elizabeth pushed back her chair and stood

up. "Somebody's tearing pages out of a book," she whispered back. "And I'm not going to let him get away with it!"

"What are you going to do?"

"I'm going to tell whoever it is to stop before any more damage is done," she said with determination.

But when Elizabeth got up, she saw that the person at the other desk—a tall, slender woman about the same age as Elizabeth's mother—had also gotten up to leave. What she held in her hand, ready to return to the reference shelf, wasn't a book; it was a newspaper.

An alarm went off in Elizabeth's head, and she stood still. Could this be the same person who cut up the newspaper she had found? It seemed unlikely, but Elizabeth decided not to confront the woman until she figured out what she had been up to.

"What's the matter?" Amy hissed. "Aren't you going to talk to her?"

Elizabeth shook her head. She watched as the woman tucked a folded piece of paper into her purse and walked out of the reference section.

"Let's look at the newspaper she was ripping up," Elizabeth whispered to Amy. She ran over to the reference shelf and picked up the newspaper she had just seen the woman put down. Quickly, she flipped through it.

"Here it is!" Elizabeth said, pointing to the page that had been torn. "It's a Los Angeles paper, a few weeks old. And there's an entire article missing, not just a word or two!"

"I wonder what the article was about," Amy mused. "It's too bad we don't have any way of finding out."

"But we do!" Elizabeth exclaimed. She checked the date on the paper, and hurried over to the reference desk. A minute later she came back with a microfilm reel in her hand.

"We're in luck!" she exclaimed. "This issue of the paper is on microfilm!"

In a rush, she explained to Amy that libraries keep older newspapers on microfilm, a sort of filmstrip of the whole paper that had to be read with a special projector. "Microfilms last much longer than newspapers," Elizabeth explained as she put the reel on the microfilm reader. "And they don't take up as much room."

Amy turned the handle of the reader while Elizabeth scanned the screen, looking for the page that the woman had torn out.

"There it is!" Elizabeth said, pointing at the screen. "Look! The article is about a kidnapping!" The headline read "KIDNAPPING STILL UNSOLVED."

Breathlessly, the girls read the article. It said that a Los Angeles family had reported to the police that their daughter had been kidnapped. They had paid the kidnapper a ransom, but their daughter hadn't been returned to them. Instead, the kidnapper had demanded even more money. At that point, since they couldn't raise any more money, the family had called the police. But by the time the police entered the case, there weren't any clues, and the kidnapper hadn't been caught or the girl found—at least, not when the article was written.

Amy sat back. "Wow," she breathed. "A real kidnapping!"

"Yes," Elizabeth said.

"Do you think," Amy whispered, "that the woman who tore out this article—"

"—is the kidnapper?" Elizabeth finished for her. She nodded slowly.

The two girls stood up at the same instant and hurried out of the main reading room of the library. But the woman was nowhere to be seen.

Six

◇

Elizabeth had invited Amy over for dinner that night. It was almost six by the time the two girls finished up at the library and got back to the Wakefields' house. Mrs. Wakefield was in the kitchen, making a huge pizza for dinner. Steven was there, too. He was reaching for a piece of cheese when Elizabeth and Amy came into the kitchen.

"Steven," Mrs. Wakefield said, "could you please save some of that for the pizza topping?"

Reluctantly, Steven put the cheese down. "Well, if there's nothing to eat," he teased his mother, "I guess I'll go shoot some baskets. I just hope I don't starve to death before dinner."

He started out of the room.

"Wait a minute, Steven," Mrs. Wakefield called after him. "I was looking for the telephone book this afternoon, and I couldn't find it. Didn't I see you with it earlier today?"

"I guess," Steven said vaguely. "Yeah, I think so. But I don't remember where I put it."

Mrs. Wakefield shook her head, frowning. "I don't know what's gotten into you lately, Steven. You seem to forget everything but mealtime."

Jessica wandered into the kitchen and overheard the conversation. "It's probably Laura," she giggled. "Every time Steven falls madly in love, he forgets everything."

Elizabeth saw that Steven's ears were starting to turn pink. "It has nothing to do with Laura," he said hotly. He scowled at Jessica. "And anyway, I haven't forgotten anything lately. I don't know what you're talking about."

"Well," Jessica said, her hands on her hips, "you forgot to write down that telephone message the other day, didn't you?"

"Message," Steven said with a smirk. "What message are you talking about?"

"See," Jessica said to Elizabeth and Amy. "He's so forgetful he can't even remember that he forgot!"

Steven gave Jessica a threatening glare. Mrs. Wakefield spoke up.

"Steven," she said, "I think there's a basketball waiting for you outside. Elizabeth, it's your turn to set the table."

Elizabeth got the dishes out of the cupboard and handed them to Amy, who was helping her. Amy and Mrs. Wakefield were discussing what the girls had learned about Mexico that day, but Elizabeth wasn't really listening. She was deep in thought. Something had occurred to her when Jessica mentioned the telephone message that Steven had forgotten. He'd said that the call had been about money. Whoever called had needed money and had to get away. Or had money and needed to get away.

At the time, Elizabeth had wondered if the telephone call might have been from Mary. Now, something new had occurred to her. If the call was from Mary, maybe the money she was talking about was ransom money! Maybe she had managed to get away from her kidnapper just long enough to get to a phone. Maybe she hadn't been able to reach her mother, and she'd tried to reach the twins, instead.

Just as Amy and Elizabeth were finishing their work in the kitchen, Jessica poked her head into the room and said, "You guys, come upstairs. I need to tell you something."

A few minutes later, the three girls were in Elizabeth's room. Jessica told Amy and Elizabeth what she and Lila and Ellen had seen that afternoon at the Wallaces'.

"Mrs. Wallace was definitely on her way to pay the ransom," Jessica said firmly. "Or at least, the first part of it. She was carrying a suitcase and some of Mary's clothes, and even Max!"

Then Elizabeth and Amy told Jessica what they had seen in the library.

"Wow," Jessica said. "I'm sure you saw Annie DeSalvo!"

"The question is, what do we do now?" Elizabeth asked grimly. "We don't have any real proof. And we can't go to the police again; they've already looked into it and they didn't come up with anything."

"That's right," Jessica said. "We're going to have to save Mary ourselves. But how?"

The girls looked at one another. Jessica was right. Saving Mary was up to them.

Seven

Since Mary was a grade ahead of the twins at school, they knew they wouldn't see her on Monday until lunchtime—if she was there at all. The morning went by slowly, and as soon as the lunch bell rang, Elizabeth and Jessica searched the cafeteria for Mary. She wasn't there.

"No luck," Elizabeth told Amy as she slid into the seat Amy had been saving for her.

"Well, I guess that settles it," Amy said with a sigh. "She's not here."

Elizabeth nodded. "I just wish we could figure out what to do."

"I'm still trying to figure out what to do about my *Sixers* article," Amy said glumly. "I gave my only copy to Mary."

"Don't worry," Elizabeth said. "We can put something else into the paper."

Amy laughed. "We could do the article that Lila suggested. Remember? About the letter she got from Donny Diamond's fan club? She even had a headline for it: 'LILA FOWLER RECEIVES LETTER FROM DONNY DIAMOND.' " She shook her head. "They're so snobby."

Elizabeth smiled. "I wouldn't mind putting something into the paper about the Unicorns. The only problem is that they never do anything worth writing about. Last week Jessica had three big ideas for stories we should put in the *Sixers*. The first one was about Lila's ice cream party, the second was about the Unicorns' trip to the mall, and the third was about Ellen's weekend in Santa Monica."

"Really exciting stuff," Amy remarked with a giggle.

"The Unicorns honestly think so," Elizabeth said. "But I'm sure no one else would agree."

"You're right," Amy said. "No one does care about Ellen's weekend in Santa Monica besides the Unicorns. And of course, they already know all about it. Hey, I have an idea. Let's write an article about the Monopoly game we played two days ago."

Elizabeth laughed. "Very funny, Amy. Just don't let Jessica hear you say that."

At a nearby table, Jessica had just joined Lila and Ellen.

"Well," Ellen said eagerly, "are there any new developments in our mystery?"

It only took Jessica a minute to tell her friends what Elizabeth and Amy had seen at the library the day before.

"I knew it!" Lila said triumphantly. "Mary has been kidnapped."

Jessica frowned slightly. She wanted to point out that it had been *her* idea that Mary had been kidnapped and Lila hadn't believed it until Jessica had proven it to her. But she decided not to.

Just then Kimberly Haver, a Unicorn who was in the seventh grade with Mary, stopped by the table. She looked concerned. "I heard a rumor," she said, "about Mary Wallace and the Unicorn treasury. Is it true that they're both missing? Lots of people are talking about it."

Jessica, Lila, and Ellen exchanged looks.

"It's true that Mary is missing," Lila confirmed importantly.

"And no one but Mary knows where the treasury is kept," Ellen said with a mysterious look.

"But," Jessica put in quickly, "Mary Wallace is a very responsible person. We're positive that there's a good explanation for her absence."

As Jessica spoke, her social studies teacher, Mrs. Arnette was walking by the table. Everybody called her "The Hairnet" because she always wore a net over her bun. As usual, she was carrying her lesson-plan book. It had been Mrs. Arnette's idea that all the social studies classes do research projects on Mexico.

"That's right, girls," Mrs. Arnette said, pausing beside them. "In fact, Mary Wallace is in Mexico."

Jessica stared, her mouth dropping open. "Me—Mexico?" she stammered.

"That's right." Mrs. Arnette beamed. "She was so excited about our project on Mexico that she decided to go there to do her research. Her mother called and told me about Mary's plans, and I was glad to give my approval. That's why she hasn't been at school for the past few days." Mrs. Arnette smiled. "We should all look forward to Mary's return," she added. "I'm sure she'll have many interesting things to tell us about her trip. See you in class, girls," she said as she turned and walked away. Kimberly smiled and went to another table, obviously reassured by what Mrs. Arnette had said.

"Mexico?" Jessica gulped, feeling confused. "But . . . how could . . ."

"Don't tell me you believed that silly story?" Lila said with a smirk.

"Right," Ellen put in. "I bet Mrs. Wallace made it up. Mary's been gone almost a week now. Her mother would have to tell the teachers something."

"Exactly," Lila said. "And don't forget what we saw yesterday. The ransom money, and the clothes and Mary's teddy bear. Those are all facts. We can't escape facts, can we?"

"Of course we can't," Jessica agreed, feeling better.

Elizabeth and Amy had ridden their bikes to school that day. After school, they stopped at the supermarket to pick up some groceries for Mrs. Sutton. Elizabeth was leafing through a magazine at the front of the store while Amy went for a loaf of bread in the back.

Suddenly, Elizabeth heard a loud whisper. "*Ps-ss-t*, Elizabeth!"

Elizabeth looked around. It sounded like Amy, but where was she?

"Elizabeth, over here!" The voice was coming from behind a cardboard cutout of a clown atop a display of cookie boxes.

Elizabeth contemplated the stack of boxes. "Is that you, Amy?" she asked, putting the magazine back on the rack. "What are you doing behind those cookie boxes?"

"I'm hiding," Amy said, still whispering. The boxes on the top of the stack shifted a little and the cardboard clown swayed from side to side. "You'd better find some place to hide, too, Elizabeth. We don't want her to see us."

"We don't want *who* to see us?" Elizabeth asked. She put out a hand to steady the clown. "Really, Amy, you'd better be careful. These boxes are about to fall over."

Amy ignored Elizabeth's warning. "Look over there by the ice cream freezer," she hissed. "That lady in the gray blouse. Isn't she the same woman we saw in the library yesterday afternoon?"

Elizabeth looked and gave a little gasp. It *was* the same woman.

"You're right, Amy," Elizabeth said. "The one Jessica thinks was Annie DeSalvo!"

"She's coming this way!" Amy exclaimed excitedly. "We can't let her see us. Get back behind these boxes, Elizabeth. Hurry!"

"Don't worry, Amy," Elizabeth replied. "That woman didn't pay any attention to us in the library yesterday. I doubt she even saw us. She doesn't have any reason to guess that we suspect her."

Amy stood up behind the cookie boxes. "I guess you're right," she whispered. Then, remembering it was safe, she cleared her throat and began to speak in her normal voice. "But what do we do now? We can't let her get away."

"Look out!" Elizabeth cried. "The boxes!"

As she watched in horror, the boxes of cookies cascaded onto the floor, burying the cardboard clown beneath them. Everybody in the store turned to look.

"Uh-oh," Amy said, biting her lip. "Now she really *will* see us!"

But the woman didn't seem to be paying any attention. The girls quickly stacked the boxes up again, keeping one eye on the woman as she went through the check-out line. By the time Amy had placed the clown securely on top of the stack of boxes, the woman had paid for her groceries and was leaving the store.

"Come on," Elizabeth said, starting toward the door.

"What are we going to do?" Amy asked.

"We're going to follow her," Elizabeth said with determination. "If she did kidnap Mary, she might lead us to wherever she's holding her."

Amy looked doubtful. "But we're riding our bikes. She's probably driving a car."

"I know. But I think we should give it a try anyway. If she drives slowly, we might be able to keep up with her. At least we'll be able to get her license-plate number."

The girls hurried through the check-out line and then went outside. The woman had just finished loading her groceries into a green car.

Quickly, Elizabeth made a note of the license-plate number. Then the girls jumped onto their bikes and pedaled after the car.

The late-afternoon traffic was heavy, so the woman couldn't drive very fast. But even so, the girls were barely able to keep her in sight. She drove into an older section of town, on the other side of Sweet Valley Middle School. After a few blocks, she turned into a driveway that was overgrown with weeds, and got out. She paused, and looked in both directions as if to make sure she hadn't been followed. Then, apparently assured that everything was safe, she took her groceries out of the car and disappeared into the house.

Elizabeth and Amy stopped across the street, laid their bikes down quietly behind some bushes, and tried to look as if they were just taking a walk around the neighborhood. The house that the woman had gone into had a long front porch and an attic. Even though it was half-hidden by shrubs and trees, Elizabeth could see that the house wasn't in good condition. Some of the shutters were off their hinges, the paint was peeling, and it looked as if the porch was about to collapse. It was a creepy house.

"Kind of spooky, isn't it?" Amy said.

"Yes," Elizabeth agreed. "It looks haunted."

"Do you think Mary is in there?" Amy asked.

"I don't know," Elizabeth said slowly. "But there's only one way to find out. Somehow, we have to get inside."

After some discussion, Elizabeth and Amy agreed on a plan. They would go home for dinner so that their parents wouldn't worry. But after dinner they would come back to the house, wait until the woman left, and then try to get in. They had to find out if Mary was inside.

After dinner that evening, Elizabeth, Jessica, and Amy were walking up the driveway to the Fowler home. The girls were all wearing dark sweaters with their jeans. Elizabeth had suggested it. She said it would make them harder to spot in the dark. If they were going to watch the old house, they had to be sure no one would discover them.

"I still don't understand," Amy said in a grouchy voice, "why Lila and Ellen have to come with us. The more people, the more chance there is that something will go wrong."

"I told you, Amy," Jessica said impatiently.

"Mary is a Unicorn. Lila and Ellen are worried about her."

"The only thing Ellen Riteman is concerned about is herself," Amy said forcefully. "She's nothing but a big chicken. I bet that as soon as she sees that creepy old haunted house, Ellen will run home."

"Stop it, Amy," Jessica said indignantly. "Don't say mean things about my friends. And don't forget that I'm a Unicorn, too. Anyway, *I* don't see why *you're* involved in this."

Amy put her hands on her hips. "Who was in the library when Annie DeSalvo ripped up the newspaper? And who saw her in the supermarket and followed her home? I did! And that's why I'm involved."

Elizabeth stepped between Jessica and Amy. "It's OK, Amy," she said reassuringly. "It certainly won't hurt to have a couple of other people with us when we go to the house. We don't know what might happen."

"Well, I guess," Amy conceded. "It's probably better to be on the safe side."

Jessica rang the doorbell of the huge, imposing Fowler mansion. Lila opened the door almost immediately. Ellen was standing behind her. Both of them were dressed in dark clothes.

"Hi," Jessica said. "Are you ready?"

Lila and Ellen glanced at each other. "We've been thinking," Ellen said. "Maybe it would be better if we didn't all go tonight." She was careful not to look at Amy. "Five people will attract too much attention. Four, on the other hand—"

"That's a great idea, Ellen," Amy said, smiling with satisfaction. "Five is way too many. Four would be much better. Anyway, I'm sure you'll be glad you don't have to go near that creepy old house." She leaned toward Ellen and lowered her voice. "Believe me, it's a spooky place. I bet there's at least one ghost in that attic, maybe more."

Ellen turned pale. "Ghosts?" she asked faintly, backing up a step. "Nobody said anything about . . ."

Lila gave Ellen a cautioning look. Then she turned to Amy.

"No, Amy," she said, "we were thinking that it would be better if *you* didn't come with us. After all, this is really Unicorn business. Of course," she added smoothly, "Elizabeth is here because she's a special friend of Mary's."

"And Amy is here," Elizabeth put in firmly, "because she's been involved since the beginning. Anyway, five people aren't likely to attract any more attention than four. At least, not if we're careful."

"Well, I suppose," Lila said, giving in. "All right, Amy, you can come with us. But you have to stick with the plan. You have to do exactly as I say, or you'll be sorry."

Amy started to say something, but Elizabeth shook her head at her. Elizabeth knew there was no use trying to argue with Lila. She liked to be in charge. Amy folded her arms and stepped back, looking grim.

"If you don't mind my asking," Elizabeth said mildly, "what *is* the plan?"

Lila rolled her eyes. "Well, I don't know yet," she said. "How could I have a plan when I haven't even seen the house yet?" She paused, glancing at each of the four other girls. She was obviously enjoying her self-appointed role as their leader. "You might call this a reconnaissance mission."

"Reconnaissance?" Ellen asked uncertainly. A worry line appeared across her forehead.

"Yeah," Jessica told her, eyes sparkling with

excitement. "We're going to look things over. You know, like spies in enemy territory. After that, we can make a plan."

"Oh," was all Ellen said.

"Then it's all settled," Lila said, sounding satisfied. She smiled at the others. "Are we ready to go?"

Jessica nodded. "Come on, everybody. There's not a minute to lose! We have to rescue Mary!"

Eight

◇

It was twilight by the time the girls got to the old house. Beside it there was a big yard filled with trees and shrubbery that hadn't been trimmed for years. A flower garden had been planted there a long time ago and thorny overgrown rosebushes concealed a narrow path. Elizabeth thought it looked like a perfect place to hide.

Lila thought so, too. She ordered them all to creep into the garden and hide behind a large hedge. The sun hadn't set yet, but under the trees, the garden was full of shadows. Crouching behind the hedge, Elizabeth could hear crickets chirping nearby.

"Ouch!" Ellen said, pushing a thorny branch out of her way. She reached up to touch her cheek. "I'm bleeding!" she cried.

"You'll survive," Amy said calmly. "A few drops of blood never hurt anybody."

"Be quiet, you two," Lila commanded in a firm whisper. "Everybody, keep your voices down. We don't want anybody to hear us." She turned to Elizabeth and pointed at the green car in the driveway of the old house. "Is that the car you followed this afternoon?"

"That's it," Elizabeth said. "The kidnapper must still be inside." She could see a light in one of the windows on the first floor. "That's probably the kitchen back there, where the light is," she added, nodding toward the back of the house. "Maybe Annie DeSalvo is cooking dinner."

Amy put her hand on Elizabeth's arm. "There's a light upstairs, too," she whispered.

Elizabeth looked up. A shade was pulled down in an upstairs window. A light shone behind it. Mary might be in that room. Elizabeth could feel her heart pounding.

"But if the kidnapper is still in the house,"

Ellen said in a loud whisper, "we can't go inside, right?"

Lila nodded firmly. "Right. We can't take the chance of being spotted by Annie DeSalvo. If she thinks somebody is spying on her, she might take Mary to another hiding place, somewhere where we'd never find them."

Ellen stood up, looking relieved. "Well, if we can't go inside, I vote that we go home. We can't help Mary from out here. And anyway, it's going to get really dark soon. I promised my mother that I—"

"Go home?" Jessica asked, looking indignantly at Ellen. "And leave Mary here, all alone? Without even letting her know that she's about to be rescued?"

"Well," Ellen said, "we'd come back later, when the kidnapper isn't here. Like tomorrow after school." She looked at the old house. "When it's *lighter*," she added.

Amy rolled her eyes at Elizabeth. "If you want to go home, Ellen," she said sweetly, "why don't you just go? Nobody will think you're a chicken."

Ellen swiveled around to face her. "What do you mean?" she demanded.

"I just meant that nobody would blame you for being scared," Amy said. "It really is a spooky old house." She put her hand on Ellen's shoulder. There was a quaver in her voice. "I just know this house is haunted, don't you?"

Ellen shuddered. Her face was pale in the twilight. She turned to Lila. "Don't you think we should leave, Lila? It's going to be dark in just a few minutes. I—"

Suddenly there was a rustling in the bushes right behind them. It sounded as if somebody, or something, was creeping through the leaves.

Amy opened her eyes very wide. "Oh, no, Ellen," she breathed. "What could that be? Do you think that there are ghosts in the garden, too?"

It was too much for Ellen. She stood up. "I don't care about the rest of you," she announced in a trembling voice, "but I'm leaving. I've had enough of this creepy old place!"

At that moment, a tabby cat, hardly any bigger than a kitten, came out of the trees. It rubbed against Elizabeth's leg, and started to purr.

"A cat." Lila laughed. "Come on, Ellen. I can't believe you're afraid of a cat."

Ellen's face was flushed. "I . . . I'm not afraid,"

she said defensively. She looked uncertainly at Lila and then at the others.

"Well then, stay," Amy said. She chuckled. "Unless, you really are scared."

Ellen sat back down, looking flustered.

"Good," Lila said. "That settles that." She glanced at the house. "Now," she said, in a voice of authority, "we need a volunteer. Somebody has to look in the kitchen window and see if Annie DeSalvo really is in there, and if there's a back door."

Elizabeth looked at the light in the upstairs window. Somehow, she knew, they had to find out if Mary was in that room. And if she was, they had to find a way to get her out.

"I'll go," Elizabeth volunteered.

"I'll go with you," Amy offered quickly.

"I'll go, too," Jessica said, after a pause. "I can't stand the thought of Mary being in that spooky house all by herself."

Ellen was silent.

"Three is too many," Lila decided. "Jessica, you stay here with Ellen and me. We'll be the lookouts."

Jessica nodded.

Elizabeth crept forward, keeping to the shad-

ows of the bushes. She could hear Amy following right behind her.

They sneaked carefully across the gravel driveway, and up to the kitchen window.

"It's too high," Elizabeth whispered. "We can't
see inside."

"You could if you stood on my back," Amy
replied. She knelt down. Elizabeth stepped onto
Amy's back and peeked over the edge of the
windowsill. Inside, she could see a woman standing at the stove, stirring something in a skillet.
It was the same woman they had seen that
afternoon. There was nobody else in the room.

Elizabeth jumped down. "It's her," she said.
"And she's alone. Let's check the back door."

The girls crept around to the back of the house.
The flight of stairs leading to the back door
was rotted through, and they could see a big
board nailed across the back door. It was clear
that the door hadn't been used in years.

"Looks like we're not going to get in through
there," Amy observed.

"No," Elizabeth agreed. "But we can get in
there." She pointed to a basement window. The
glass had fallen out of it. "It wouldn't be hard to
climb through the window," Elizabeth whispered.

"And there must be a way to get upstairs from the basement."

Amy shivered. "That really does look scary— even to me," she said, looking at the dark basement window.

"It does," Elizabeth agreed. She could feel the goose bumps rising on her arms. "But it may be our only chance."

They stared at the dark window for a few more seconds, and then Amy whispered, "Come on, let's get out of here."

The two girls crept quietly back to join Jessica, Lila, and Ellen. Elizabeth was reporting what they had found when suddenly Amy clutched her arm.

"Look!" she hissed. She was pointing at the upstairs window.

Elizabeth looked. Another light had been turned on in the room upstairs. Now she could see two dark silhouettes against the shade. One, tall and slender, was standing and moving around. A smaller figure was seated, and not moving at all.

"It's the kidnapper!" Ellen said hoarsely, holding on to Lila.

"And Mary!" Jessica exclaimed. "That's Mary up there!"

The girls watched in silence for a few minutes, while the tall figure moved around the room. The seated figure still didn't move.

"She's probably tied to a chair or something," Jessica said.

Elizabeth nodded. "And the kidnapper is giving her something to eat."

After another few minutes, the light went out. The two silhouettes disappeared, although there was still a faint light on in the room. After a while, a light went on in one of the front rooms downstairs.

Elizabeth glanced at her watch. She could barely make out the time because it was so dark in the garden. "It's almost eight o'clock," she said. "Jessica and I have to go home." It was getting late, and she didn't want her parents to worry.

"I do, too," Ellen said.

Lila silenced her with a fierce look. "Well, if we have to go, we have to go," she said. "Anyway, it doesn't look like the kidnapper is going anywhere tonight, and that means we can't get into the house. We'll have to come again tomorrow night. Let's meet at the corner at six-thirty."

Ellen whispered something to Lila, but Lila

answered in a voice loud enough for them all to hear. "It's OK, Ellen," she said. "I think we ought to let Amy come, too."

Amy looked at Ellen. "Of course, *you* don't have to come if you don't want to, Ellen," she said. "I mean, if you have something more important to do, we'll understand."

Ellen gave her a defiant look. "I'll be here," she said.

"Fine," Lila said. She looked around. "Everybody, be on time. I don't want anybody to be late. And don't forget to wear something dark."

"We'll be on time," Jessica assured her. They all agreed.

Nine

◇

"Come on, Jessica, hurry up," Lila said urgently. "The others will be waiting."

It was nearly six-thirty the following evening. Jessica had eaten dinner at Lila's house, and the two were on their way to the corner where they were supposed to meet Elizabeth, Ellen, and Amy. They were late.

"I'm hurrying," Jessica snapped, pushing her hair out of her eyes. She was angry at Lila. They were late because Lila had called Bruce Patman, the cutest boy in seventh grade, on the phone after dinner. Jessica had talked to him briefly, but Lila had talked to him for what seemed like forever, even when Jessica had pointed out that they were going to be late if Lila didn't get off the phone.

Now, they were walking very fast, up a long, steep hill. Jessica was out of breath. Suddenly, Lila stopped.

"What's the matter?" Jessica snapped. "Why are you stopping, Lila? We're in a hurry, remember?"

"I'm stopping," Lila said angrily, "because the heel came off of my shoe." She took off her leather sandal and held it up. "You can't expect me to go barefoot," she said. "Find me a rock, and I'll see if I can pound it back on."

"But we're late!" Jessica exclaimed. "Elizabeth, Amy, and Ellen are probably there already, waiting for us! And you made a big deal about being on time. I bet they'll be really mad at us."

"I know!" Lila said impatiently. She sat down on the curb and scowled at her shoe. "If you hadn't talked to Bruce for so long, we might have been on time."

"Me?" Jessica asked. There was a rock in a nearby flower bed and she bent down to pick it up.

"You talked to him much longer than I did, Lila. I kept telling you we had to go, but you didn't pay any attention."

Lila sighed. "Well, it doesn't matter now," she said. She took the rock Jessica handed her. She pounded on the heel of her sandal, put her foot back into it and stood up. "There," she said. "Maybe it will stay on now."

"I hope so," Jessica said. She looked up the hill. "We still have a long way to go. Maybe if we run—"

"If you think I'm going to run all the way there," Lila said, "you're wrong. Anyway, if I run, my heel might come off again. We'll just have to be late, that's all." She began to walk. "When we explain, I'm sure the others will understand."

"I wonder where Lila is," Ellen said, looking at her watch. She and Amy were waiting on the corner, across the street from the old house. It would be dark in a little while.

"Don't worry," Amy said. "It's not even six-thirty yet. Lila will be here, sooner or later. She wouldn't miss a chance to give orders."

"Maybe Lila decided she had better things to

do than hang out with *you*," Ellen said, lifting her nose.

Amy shrugged, and squinted at Ellen. "Actually, I'm surprised to see you here, Ellen. I thought your mom would need you for something important tonight. Or that you'd get sick or you'd forget—"

"You stop that, Amy Sutton," Ellen shouted angrily. "You make me so mad!"

Just at that moment, Elizabeth walked up. "Hi," she said.

"Hi," Amy replied. "I'm glad you're here. Did you have any trouble getting away tonight?"

"No, but Jessica and I have to be home by eight-thirty." She looked around. "Where is Jessica?" she asked. "And Lila?"

"They're not here yet," Amy reported.

"That's strange," Elizabeth said. "Jessica—"

But Elizabeth didn't get to finish her sentence. "Look!" Ellen said in a hushed voice, interrupting her. Across the street, the kidnapper came out of the house and locked the front door carefully. "Hide!" Ellen screeched frantically. "She'll see us!"

But the woman wasn't paying attention to

them. Without even so much as a glance in their direction, she got into the green car. A moment later, she backed out of the drive and headed down the street.

"That was close," Ellen said with a sigh of relief. "I was afraid—" She glanced at Amy. "I mean, who knows what that woman might do? A kidnapper could be very dangerous."

Elizabeth's eyes followed the departing car. "I wonder where she's going," she said thoughtfully. She shook her head. "I wish Jessica and Lila were here, so we could decide what to do next."

Ellen looked at her watch again. "Where *are* they?" she asked. "If Lila were here, she could tell us what to do."

"Well, I don't think we should wait any longer," Amy said. "We have to go into the house and get Mary out while we've got a chance."

"But what if the kidnapper comes back and catches us?" Ellen protested. "There's no telling what she might do to us!"

Amy gave her a disgusted look. "Ellen Riteman, there is no doubt about it. You are the biggest chicken I've ever met."

"I am not!" Ellen yelled.

"You are too!" Amy yelled back.

Elizabeth spoke up. "I can't believe you two. Amy, what do you think we should do?" she asked.

"Well, we need someone to go into the house for Mary," Amy replied, "and someone to wait out here for Jessica and Lila."

"What if two of us go in," Elizabeth said. "And the other waits here for them?"

"That sounds good," Amy said. "But we'd better do it now. If we stand here arguing about it any longer, Annie DeSalvo might come back." She shivered. "I don't think I'd like to be in there when she does."

"So what we have to decide," Elizabeth said, "is who will go inside the house and who will wait outside."

"Ha!" Amy said shortly. "Who do you think will go in? You and me, that's who."

"What do you say, Ellen?" Elizabeth asked. There was no answer. She turned around. "Ellen?"

"Ellen?" Amy asked, looking over her shoulder.

But Ellen was nowhere to be seen. For a moment, Elizabeth and Amy stared at each other in silence.

"Do you think she went home?" Elizabeth asked.

"She couldn't have gotten far. We'd still be able to see her," Amy replied.

"But then where . . ." Elizabeth asked.

They looked at each other again, not saying anything. Then, at the same instant, they both broke into a run. They dashed across the street and down the driveway toward the back of the house. As they came around the corner by the back door, they caught a glimpse of Ellen. She was disappearing through the basement window!

"I don't believe it," Amy said, shaking her head in amazement. "I don't believe that Ellen just went through that window."

"She probably got tired of listening to you call her a chicken," Elizabeth replied. "So she decided to prove that she wasn't."

Amy scowled. "Well, that was pretty stupid. What does she think she can do in there all by herself?"

"I don't think Ellen ought to be in there all by herself," Elizabeth said. "She might need help."

Amy sucked in her breath. "You're right, Elizabeth."

Then, before Elizabeth could stop her, Amy headed toward the basement window. "You wait for Jessica and Lila," she said. "I'll go find Ellen."

And as Elizabeth watched, with her heart in her mouth, Amy disappeared through the basement window and into the gloomy old house.

Ten

◇

The basement was pitch dark when Amy got inside. It smelled musty, as if it hadn't been used for years. It was too dark to see, but Amy imagined that there were spiders all over the place, and that the walls were covered with cobwebs. A shiver ran down her spine. It wasn't exactly the kind of place she wanted to be in alone.

"Ellen," she said, in a loud whisper. She put her hand out into the darkness. "Ellen, where are you?"

But the only reply was a faint rustling in one

corner, and goose bumps popped out on Amy's arms. Probably a rat, she thought.

Now that her eyes were getting used to the dark, she could see a little better. Ahead in the dimness, she could make out a staircase. At the top, there was a crack of light under a door. Holding her breath, she crept up the shaky stairs, touching the splintery railing only when she had to. Cautiously, she opened the door and peeked out. She could see a deserted hall that was lit only by a small lamp sitting on a table.

"Ellen!" Amy whispered again. Still no answer. She stepped carefully into the hallway, closing the door to the basement behind her. At one end, there was a dark, empty kitchen. At the other end was the stairway. The living room was at that end of the hall, too, its furniture looming black and bulky in the weak light. Amy walked down the hall, and hesitated at the doorway to survey the living room.

"Ellen, are you in here?" she called.

Suddenly, upstairs, Amy heard a crash and what sounded like a muffled cry. At that very moment, a pair of lights swung into the driveway outside, lighting the living room with a bright glare. It was the kidnapper! She had come back! Without thinking, Amy jumped for the nearest safe place, behind the sofa. She crouched there, trembling, as the woman slammed the car door, walked swiftly up the porch steps, and unlocked the front door. The door squeaked loudly as she closed and locked it behind her. Then her footsteps clicked down the hallway and into the kitchen.

Amy held her breath, shivering. She couldn't get out the front door without being heard. She couldn't get to the basement stairs without being seen. She was trapped!

Outside, Elizabeth stood staring at the house. The kidnapper was back! Elizabeth had seen the green car pull into the drive. Then the woman had hurried into the house, carrying something. A moment later, the light in the kitchen had gone on. And Jessica and Lila still hadn't arrived.

Elizabeth hesitated, not sure what she should do. Maybe she should go to the door and ring the bell. If she distracted the kidnapper long enough, Amy and Ellen might have a chance to get out of the house through the basement window. Maybe they could even take Mary with them. But before she could think of an excuse for ringing the bell, she heard footsteps behind her.

"Hi, Liz," Jessica said breathlessly. "Sorry we're late."

Elizabeth jumped and turned around. "Jessica!" she exclaimed. "Where have you been?"

"The heel came off Lila's shoe," Jessica explained. She stopped to catch her breath. "She had to fix it."

Lila was standing behind Jessica. "Actually, if Jessica hadn't talked to Bruce Patman on the phone for such a long time," she added, "we could have started sooner." Lila was breathless, too.

"I don't know what you're talking about, Lila," Jessica said. "You talked longer than I did. And it was your idea to call him in the first place, remember?"

Lila ignored her. "Where's Ellen?" she asked Elizabeth. "And Amy? Are they late?"

"They're in the house," Elizabeth said, shaking her head. She was angry with Jessica and Lila for being late, but there was no time to discuss it now. It would just waste precious time. "The kidnapper left, and Ellen went in first, by herself," she said. "Amy went in to help her. Then the kidnapper came back!"

"Ellen went in by herself?" Jessica asked. "Into that creepy old house?"

Lila scowled. "What a dumb thing to do. Now we're split up. We should have stayed together until we decided what to do."

"Well, we weren't all here to decide," Elizabeth retorted. She looked at the house. The light was still on in the kitchen, and she could see somebody moving around. "I think we ought to go inside."

Lila nodded. "You go. I'll go call the police," she said authoritatively. "Jessica, you come with me."

Jessica shook her head. "I think I should stick with Elizabeth," she said. "You go call the police, Lila. No, wait, maybe you'd better come with us. If we have to fight off the kidnapper, you might be useful."

Lila shifted uncomfortably. "We ought to be able to come up with a better plan."

Elizabeth stared at her. "Well, what then?"

"I'm thinking, I'm thinking," Lila muttered. "Give me a minute, will you?"

But a minute came and went, and then two

minutes, then three. And still Lila hadn't come up with a better plan.

Inside, Amy was still hiding behind the sofa, crouched down, hardly breathing. She listened to the woman moving around in the kitchen. The refrigerator door opened and bottles clinked. It sounded like the kidnapper was putting something away. Soft drinks, maybe. Then the water in the sink was turned on. Amy figured that the kidnapper must be washing dishes.

Amy took a deep breath. Ellen had to be upstairs. Anyway, Mary was upstairs. And the kidnapper was busy in the kitchen. It was now or never. She slowly crept out from behind the sofa, and keeping to the shadows as much as she could, tiptoed out of the living room, across the dark hallway, and up the creaky old stairs. She took one stair at a time, very quietly, careful not to make even the slightest sound. A minute or two later, she had made it to the top.

She stood peering down the dimly lit hallway that stretched the length of the house. There were two doors. Amy thought carefully. It had to be the door on the right—that would be the bedroom they had seen from the garden. That's where Mary was tied up. Amy tiptoed down the hall to the door and pushed it open. It gave a long, slow squeak, very loud in the silence. Amy held her breath. Her heart was pounding like a hammer in her chest. Surely the kidnapper had heard the noise!

But apparently, Annie DeSalvo hadn't heard anything. The water in the sink was still running. Amy let out her breath with a little *whoosh,* pushed the bedroom door open the rest of the way, and stepped in.

She was greeted by a frightened gasp.

Amy stopped in the doorway. Ellen sat on the floor. There was a bruise over one of her eyes. Beside her on the floor was an overturned chair. One leg had come off and the back of the chair was broken. The crash Amy had heard must have been the chair breaking.

"Amy?" Ellen cried gratefully. "I'm so glad to see you!"

Amy knelt down. *"Ssh,"* she commanded in a stern whisper. "What happened?"

"There was a chair across the door," Ellen said, her voice trembling. "Like a booby trap or something. When I came in, I fell over it." She put her hand to her forehead with a moan. "Ooh, Amy, it hurts!"

Amy felt Ellen's head with her fingers. "It's just a little bump, that's all. You'll be fine when the swelling goes down." She looked around. "Where's Mary?"

But Ellen didn't have time to answer. Both of them heard the noise at the same time. Footsteps—coming up the stairs!

"The kidnapper's coming!" Ellen whispered, horror-struck. She grabbed Amy's arm. "What are we going to do?"

The kidnapper's footsteps were getting closer. The girls could hear them coming down the long hall. Step, step, step . . .

Amy got to her feet. "Come on!" she said, tugging at Ellen's hand. "We've got to hide. There's only one place—the closet!"

Groggily, Ellen got up. Amy raced across the room and jerked open the closet door.

"Come on!" she hissed. "Hurry, Ellen!"

But Ellen couldn't move fast enough. As Amy slipped into the closet, pulling the door almost shut behind her, the bedroom door creaked open. Holding her breath, Amy watched through the crack in the door as a hand reached around the door frame, felt around on the wall, and then turned on the light switch. On a table beside the window, a lamp came on.

Ellen stood in the middle of the room, blinking in the sudden light. The kidnapper was almost as stunned as Ellen was. She gasped. Then she dropped the glass she had been carrying. As it hit the floor, it shattered with a loud noise.

As Amy watched, helpless, Ellen whirled and ran to the window. She yanked up the shade and began to tug desperately at the window sash. She was trying to open it, but the window wouldn't go up. The old wooden sash was stuck.

The kidnapper made a fierce noise that sounded like a snarl. She hurled herself across the room at Ellen, knocking her to the floor. As Ellen fell, she crashed into the table and the light went out. The room was suddenly pitch black.

In the darkness, Amy couldn't make anything out. Then she heard the sound of a struggle. And then Ellen screamed, a long, shrill scream that sent shivers up Amy's spine.

Eleven

Outside the old house, Ellen's frightened scream shattered the silence. A few seconds before, Ellen had appeared at the upstairs window. Almost immediately, she had disappeared again, and the light in the room had gone out.

"What's happening?" Lila croaked, terrified. "What's going on?"

"Ellen's in trouble!" Elizabeth exclaimed. "The kidnapper must have found her." She started to run toward the house. "Come on! We have to save them!"

"Wait! Shouldn't we call the police?" Lila asked.

She was poised to run in the opposite direction. "The police will know what to do!"

"No, no," Jessica cried, catching Lila's arm. "It's too far to the nearest phone. There's no time for the police! Anyway, we may need your help!"

"But I don't want to go into that creepy old house!" Lila wailed.

"Well, *we're* going," Elizabeth said shortly. "Come on, Jess!"

With a last look at Lila, Jessica followed Elizabeth. The twins raced across the drive and around the back of the house.

Jessica went in through the basement window first. Elizabeth was about to follow, when suddenly she felt a hand clutching at her arm. She spun around. It was Lila. Her face was pale and her lower lip was trembling.

"I can't stay back there in the dark by myself," Lila said. "I'm coming with you."

Elizabeth nodded. "OK, then you can go in next," she said.

Lila looked at the small cobweb-covered window. "Through *there*?" she asked doubtfully. "But it's *filthy*!"

Elizabeth gave her a push. "Hurry," she said urgently.

Lila gritted her teeth and disappeared through the window. Then there was a thump and a muffled squeal.

"Ow!" Jessica cried. "Get off me, Lila!"

"Why were you sitting under the window when you knew I was coming in?" Lila asked indignantly, scrambling to her feet and dusting herself off.

"*Ssh!*" Elizabeth commanded. "You're making too much noise."

"It's dark down here," Lila complained. "I can't see a thing." She put her hand out and started to feel around.

Elizabeth pointed at a sliver of light. "Look, you guys, that must be the basement door, up there. Come on." She began to feel her way along the wall toward the light.

"But I can't see where I'm going," Lila grumbled.

"Feel your way along the wall," Elizabeth told her.

There was a brief silence as the girls inched toward the stairs, and then Lila gave a strangled wail.

"What is it, Lila?" Jessica asked.

"Cobwebs!" Lila cried. "I've got cobwebs all over my hands." She moaned. "They're in my hair, too. Ugh, I *hate* spiders! They're gross."

"*Ssh!*" Elizabeth hissed. "Don't worry about the spiders. They won't hurt you. We've got to be quiet!"

"Anyway, you're headed in the wrong direction, Lila," Jessica told her. "The stairs are over here."

"Oh," Lila said, trying to pick the cobwebs off her hands. "Where?"

"Over here," Elizabeth said patiently. "Come on."

Groping her way, Elizabeth went up the rickety stairs, followed closely by Jessica and Lila. When she got to the top, she pushed the door open a little and peered through the crack. The hallway was empty. It was dark, too. Even the kitchen light was out.

"What do you see?" Jessica asked.

"Is the kidnapper there?" Lila whispered fearfully.

"It's too dark to see anything," Elizabeth said. She listened. "I don't hear anything, either." She stepped out into the hallway.

"Well," Lila said, "I'm just happy we're getting out of that pitch black basement."

"Yeah, but it's pitch black up here, too," Jessica muttered, feeling around for Elizabeth. "Lizzie, where are you?"

There was no answer.

Lila let out a little gasp. "Jessica! Do you suppose the kidnapper—"

Jessica put her hand over Lila's mouth. "Be quiet!" she hissed. "Do you want to give us away?" She leaned out into the hall. "Elizabeth, are you there?" she whispered. Jessica felt goose bumps raising on her arms. *How could Liz disappear so quickly?* she wondered frantically.

"Lizzie?" she whispered again. Her voice was beginning to shake.

"Here I am," Elizabeth said, appearing out of the shadows. "I found the stairs to the second floor. They're over here."

Jessica sighed, and gave her sister a quick hug.

"Good work, Elizabeth," she said.

"Come on," Elizabeth said, "I'll show you the way."

Slowly, the girls crept down the hallway. Then,

in single file with Elizabeth in the lead, the girls cautiously climbed the stairs. When they got to the top, they stopped.

"Which door?" Jessica asked.

"That one," Lila said, pointing to the door on the left.

"No," Elizabeth said. "It's that one. On the right. That's the room we could see from outside."

Moving as quietly as they could, they went to the door. Gingerly, Elizabeth pushed it open. It gave a long, slow creak. Beside her, Elizabeth felt Jessica flinch. Behind Jessica, Lila pulled in her breath sharply.

Cautiously, Elizabeth peered through the open door. But she still couldn't hear or see anything. Slowly, she reached around the door and felt for the light switch. But before she could find it, the light came on. Ellen was picking up the lamp and putting it on the table.

"Ellen!" Lila and Jessica screamed at the same time. "Ellen, are you OK?" Elizabeth asked.

"Yes, I'm—" Ellen began.

"Wait!" Elizabeth interrupted her. "Where's Amy?"

"Over here," Amy said calmly.

When Elizabeth turned toward her friend, she could hardly believe what she saw. Amy was sitting on the floor on the other side of the room. Actually, she was sitting *on* the kidnapper, who was stretched out flat. The kidnapper seemed to be unconscious. Amy was holding what looked like a chair leg in her hand.

"Oh, I'm so glad to see you!" Ellen cried. "I was so scared!" She rushed over to Lila. "Lila, you won't believe how brave Amy was. The kidnapper was about to kill me when—"

"Oh, I don't think she was going to kill you," Amy said. "I think she just wanted to get you away from the window."

"She was about to kill me," Ellen rushed on, hardly taking a breath, "when Amy whacked her on the back of the head with this enormous piece of—"

"Actually, it was only a chair leg," Amy said mildly.

"—with this chair leg and knocked her out!" Ellen said. "Amy ought to get an award for being the bravest person in the world. I mean, that kidnapper was going to— If Amy hadn't—"

Lila took Ellen by the shoulders and shook her. "Ellen," she commanded, "stop babbling."

Ellen closed her mouth.

Lila turned to the others. "We have to call the police," she said. "Ellen and I are going downstairs to find a phone," she announced, grabbing Ellen and practically dragging her out of the room.

Ellen cast an admiring glance at Amy, who was still sitting on the kidnapper. "I'll stay here and help Amy," she said, prying herself loose.

Lila shrugged and left the room.

Elizabeth looked around. "Where's Mary?" she asked.

The remaining four girls looked at one another. In the excitement, they had forgotten all about Mary.

Then they spotted her, in a dark alcove. She was tied to a chair, facing the wall. Her mouth was gagged.

"Mary!" the girls shrieked at once, and rushed to her.

But when they turned the chair around and began to untie the girl's hands, they got the shock of their lives. The girl in the chair wasn't

Mary! She had red hair and blue eyes. They had never seen her before!

Elizabeth pulled the gag out of the girl's mouth while Ellen untied the ropes and handed them to Amy so she could tie up the kidnapper.

"Who are you?" Elizabeth asked the girl.

The girl looked at them with big eyes. "My name is Becky," she said, rubbing her wrists. "Becky Kern. I'm from Los Angeles. That woman kidnapped me. She was holding me until my parents paid her a ransom. How did you know I was here?"

"We thought you were our friend Mary Wallace!" Jessica said. "She's been missing, too. We thought that a woman named Annie DeSalvo had kidnapped her."

Elizabeth explained to Becky about how Mary had been missing and about how they had found the newspaper and seen the kidnapper in the library. She even explained that Mary had been kidnapped by Annie DeSalvo before.

"Annie DeSalvo?" Becky repeated. "That woman's name is Rita Partman. I saw it on an envelope that fell out of her purse."

Just then, Lila burst into the room. "The police will be here any minute," she announced.

"I told them that I'd just captured a dangerous kidnapper and—"

Amy put her hands on her hips. "*You* captured the kidnapper?" she exclaimed, sticking out her chin. "Ellen and I captured the kidnapper, Lila, in case you've forgotten. Elizabeth and I recognized her and tracked her here. And Jessica and Elizabeth pieced together the ransom note. Just exactly where do you fit into the picture?"

Ellen glanced at Amy. Then she scowled at Lila. "That's right, Lila," she said, straightening her shoulders. "What makes you think—"

Lila held up her hand. "OK, OK, Ellen," she said soothingly. She glanced toward Becky and her eyes got big. "Who are you?" she asked. "And where's Mary?"

The whereabouts of Mary Wallace was a question that not even the police could answer.

"Mary Wallace?" the police sergeant asked in response to Elizabeth's question. Looking puzzled, he turned to the officer with him. "Do we have a missing-person report out on a Mary Wallace?"

The officer, who had just finished writing down

the story Lila had told him, turned around. "Mary Wallace? Never heard of her." He gave Amy an admiring look. "I must say, young lady, that you showed remarkable bravery here tonight."

A flashbulb popped, and a young woman reporter from the *Sweet Valley News* stepped forward. "I agree," she told Amy warmly. "That kidnapper might have gotten away with another terrible crime if it hadn't been for you."

Amy grinned and put her arm around Elizabeth. "Elizabeth Wakefield was the one who figured out the kidnapper's note," she said, "and she was with me when we spotted Rita Partman in the library. And Ellen Riteman had the courage to come into the house all by herself, looking for our friend."

"But you were the one who captured the kidnapper," Ellen insisted. "That took even *more* courage."

Amy looked pleased. "Let's just say we're a good team."

"Well," Lila said angrily, coming forward and standing next to the newspaper reporter, "what about us? I was the one who phoned the police." She grabbed Jessica's arm and pulled her over. "And Jessica Wakefield helped, too." She smiled at the photographer and tossed her hair over one shoulder. "Perhaps you'd like another picture."

"The kid's right, Sam," the reporter said. "You'd better get a picture."

Lila smiled her biggest smile as the photographer pointed his camera at her.

"No, no," the reporter said crossly, "I want a picture of Amy Sutton and Elizabeth Wakefield. They're the ones who broke this thing."

Seeing the look on Lila's face, Elizabeth couldn't help smiling.

"*Well!*" Lila exclaimed furiously, and stalked away. Elizabeth expected Ellen to follow Lila, but she just stood there, watching Amy. When the reporter and the photographer were finished, Ellen approached Amy and Elizabeth.

"My mother is downstairs, waiting for me," she said. "Do you want a ride home, Amy?"

"That's OK," Amy said. "Elizabeth already offered me a ride. I can go with the Wakefields."

"But I *want* to give you a ride," Ellen pleaded. "Please?"

For a second, Elizabeth thought Amy was going to laugh. But she only shrugged and turned to

Elizabeth. "If you don't mind," she said suppressing a giggle, "I guess I'll go with Ellen."

Elizabeth nodded. "Sure," she said, and smiled as she watched Ellen follow Amy through the door.

"I guess we really caught a kidnapper," Jessica said as she and Elizabeth went down the stairs together. "Pretty neat, isn't it?"

"Yes," Elizabeth said. "But we still haven't solved the mystery. I wonder where Mary could be?"

Twelve

◇

"Mexico!" the twins gasped. They stared at Mary. She was standing on their front doorstep, wearing a flowing Mexican skirt, and looking very tanned and happy.

"Mary!" Elizabeth exclaimed. "I can't believe it!"

"Well, it's true." Mary smiled. "I've been to Mexico. With Mr. and Mrs. Altman."

"So Mrs. Arnette was right!" Jessica said. She shook her head. "I can't believe that you went all the way to Mexico just to work on a social studies report!"

Mary laughed. "Are you kidding? Of course, that was part of it. But I got in a lot of good hours on the beach, too."

"But how . . . who . . . ?" Jessica asked.

"Mom and I weren't getting along very well. I told you, remember?" Mary said.

The twins nodded, and Mary went on.

"Mr. and Mrs. Altman—you remember, my former foster parents—well, they were going to Mexico to visit some friends, and they suggested that what Mom and I needed was a little vacation from each other. So they asked me to go with them. I only had a couple of hours to get ready. I called and left a message with Steven that I was going away. I told him to tell you that the amount in the Unicorn treasury was—"

"Then it was you who called!" Elizabeth said.

Mary nodded.

"It figures," Jessica said. "Steven forgot to tell us about your call, and when he remembered, he got it all messed up."

Elizabeth sighed. "We're really glad you're back," she said.

"Thanks, Elizabeth," Mary said with a smile. Then she turned to Jessica. "There's forty-nine dollars and ten cents in the Unicorn treasury. Do you think that's enough for a party?"

Jessica nodded slowly. "I guess." She scratched her head. "You know, there's something I still haven't figured out. If your mother wasn't carrying ransom money in that suitcase, what was she carrying?"

Mary's mouth fell open. "Ransom? My mother was paying a ransom?" Mary looked from Elizabeth to Jessica. "I think," she said, "that you'd better tell me the whole story. From the beginning."

The twins proceeded to tell Mary the entire story, including the part about the police coming and taking the kidnapper away to jail, and questioning them.

When the girls were finished with their story, Mary sat for a few minutes in stunned silence. "All *that* happened while I was gone?" she finally said, "and I missed it?"

Jessica smiled. "That's what you get for going to Mexico without telling us."

Elizabeth gave Jessica a poke in the ribs. "She did try, you know, Jess," she said.

Mary laughed. "Well, I can answer your question about the ransom, I guess. Mom told me that she put a bunch of my old clothes, things that were too small for me, into a suitcase and took them to church for the bazaar."

Jessica rolled her eyes. "So that's what she meant when she told the person on the phone that she was bringing 'small stuff.' "

"And she probably made sure that the clothes didn't have any name tags on them," Elizabeth said. "That's why she said they were unmarked."

"And Max?" Jessica asked. "Where was she taking Max?"

"That's easy," Mary said with a huge grin. "Max was really filthy. Mom thought it would be a good idea to take him to the cleaners while I was gone. You should see him. He looks really spiffy!" She leaned forward. "You know, I actually spent a whole week away from Max!"

"I can't wait to tell Lila and Ellen about this," Jessica said. "They won't believe it."

"I'm glad Mary is finally back from Mexico," Lila told Jessica and Ellen. "And that our money is safe. Now we can plan our party."

The three girls were sitting out in the Wakefields' backyard a few days after Mary had come home. Surrounding them were stacks of magazines, bottles of suntan lotion, and glasses of lemonade.

"I've been thinking," Ellen said slowly, "that it would be a very good idea if we invited Amy Sutton to the party."

"Amy Sutton!" Lila exclaimed. "Why would we want to invite her? She's not a Unicorn!"

"I know she isn't," Ellen said, sort of regretfully. "But she *did* save me from being attacked by—"

"I don't want to hear any more about that," Lila said firmly. "Really, Ellen, all you can talk about lately is Amy Sutton and how she saved your life."

"But it's true!" Ellen protested. "She saved me from—"

"Not another word!" Lila almost screamed.

Ellen frowned at Lila, but she didn't say anything.

"Jessica," Lila said, changing the subject, "have you spoken to Elizabeth about the *Sixers*?"

Jessica sighed to herself. With all the excitement over Mary's disappearance, Lila had forgotten about the newspaper. That had suited Jessica just fine. Now that the mystery was solved, Jessica knew there was no way to stop

Lila from getting her way. "The *Sixers*? I don't—" Jessica began in an innocent tone.

"You didn't forget, did you?" Lila said with great urgency. "You're supposed to tell Elizabeth we want more stories about the Unicorns in *our* class newspaper."

"Oh, yeah," Jessica said. "Well, I've been too busy catching kidnappers to have time to say anything to her."

Lila nodded. "Well, you'll just have to talk to her tonight. I want there to be something about the Unicorns in the very next edition of the *Sixers*. And not just a little story, either," she added. "We need something that covers *all* our activities. After all, the Unicorns are the most important people at Sweet Valley Middle School. Right, Ellen?"

But Ellen hadn't been listening. "Jessica," she said, "do you think Amy would rather have an outdoor party by the pool or one at the skating rink?"

Jessica and Lila just looked at each other and rolled their eyes.

"Lila's right, you know," Jessica said to Elizabeth that night, while the twins were doing their homework at the kitchen table. "The *Sixers* never prints anything about the Unicorns."

"I know," Elizabeth said with a sigh. She put down her pencil. "But the Unicorns never do anything that people would want to read about."

Jessica stared at Elizabeth indignantly. "Don't you think everyone would want to read Lila's letter from the Donny Diamond Fan Club?"

Elizabeth laughed. "Well, no, not really. But, if you and Lila got an interview with Donny Diamond himself, that would be different."

"Come on," Jessica said desperately, "couldn't you find a little room in the paper for something about the Unicorns? I mean, the *Sixers* is a class newspaper, and the Unicorns are members of the class, just like everybody else."

Elizabeth frowned thoughtfully. "You're right, Jess," she said after a pause. "Maybe you ought to write a short article about the Unicorns. How about an update of all the latest news."

Jessica clapped her hands. "Oh, Lizzie, that's a great idea! The Unicorns will be so pleased!"

"But you have to keep it to two hundred words. That's all the room I can give you."

"Two hundred words!" Jessica exclaimed. "But how can I tell about the Donny Diamond letter and the ice cream party and the trip to the mall and Ellen's trip to Santa Monica in just two hundred words?"

Elizabeth shrugged. "That's my best offer," she said.

"OK. I'll take it," Jessica grumbled. "But I don't see how I can put everything into just two hundred words."

"Maybe you shouldn't try to put everything in," Elizabeth advised her. "Just pick the important things. You could leave out Ellen's trip to Santa Monica."

"But that will upset Ellen."

"OK. Then leave out the part about the Donny Diamond Fan Club letter."

"But *that* will make Lila furious," Jessica wailed.

Elizabeth laughed. "It isn't going to be easy," she said sympathetically. "But I'm sure you'll figure it out. Maybe some of the Unicorns can help you. That way, you won't have to take all of the blame if some of the Unicorns don't like the way the article turns out."

Jessica nodded. "Don't worry, I'll get the story written," she said. "And you promise that you'll put it into the next *Sixers*?"

"I promise," Elizabeth said. "I'll even try to make room for it on the front page."

"Great!" Jessica exclaimed. She jumped up to go call Lila. In the next edition of the *Sixers*, the Unicorns would be front-page news!

Will the Unicorns make headlines? Find out in Sweet Valley Twins #37, **THE WAR BETWEEN THE TWINS.**

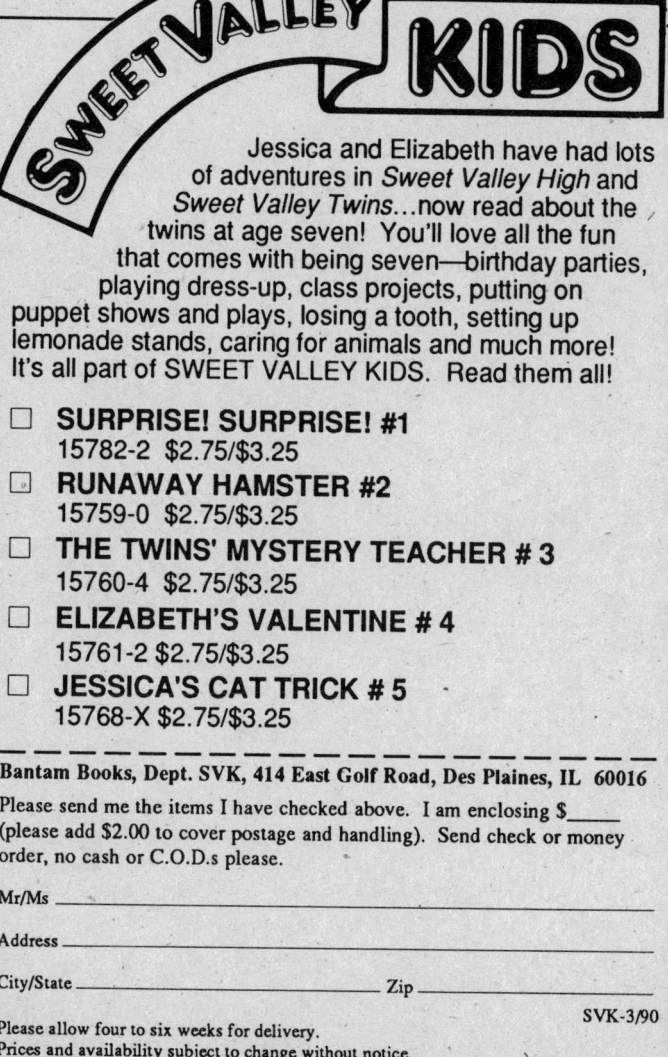

Super Books!

Join Jessica and Elizabeth for big adventure in exciting SWEET VALLEY TWINS SUPER EDITIONS and SWEET VALLEY TWINS CHILLERS. From a class trip to a search for a long-lost sister to summer camp, you'll love the fun and excitement!

- ☐ #1: CLASS TRIP 15588-1/$2.95
- ☐ #2: HOLIDAY MISCHIEF 15641-1/$2.95
- ☐ #3: THE BIG CAMP SECRET 15707-8/$2.95

CHILLERS

- ☐ #1: THE CHRISTMAS GHOST 15767-1/$2.95

SWEET VALLEY TWINS

☐ BEST FRIENDS #1 ....15655/$2.75
☐ TEACHER'S PET #2 ....15656/$2.75
☐ THE HAUNTED HOUSE #3 ....15657/$2.75
☐ CHOOSING SIDES #4 ....15658/$2.75
☐ SNEAKING OUT #5 ....15659/$2.75
☐ THE NEW GIRL #6 ....15660/$2.75
☐ THREE'S A CROWD #7 ....15661/$2.75
☐ FIRST PLACE #8 ....15662/$2.75
☐ AGAINST THE RULES #9 ....15676/$2.75
☐ ONE OF THE GANG #10 ....15677/$2.75
☐ BURIED TREASURE #11 ....15692/$2.75
☐ KEEPING SECRETS #12 ....15538/$2.50
☐ STRETCHING THE TRUTH #13 ....15654/$2.75
☐ TUG OF WAR #14 ....15663/$2.75
☐ THE OLDER BOY #15 ....15664/$2.75
☐ SECOND BEST #16 ....15665/$2.75
☐ BOYS AGAINST GIRLS #17 ....15666/$2.75
☐ CENTER OF ATTENTION #18 ....15668/$2.75
☐ THE BULLY #19 ....15667/$2.75
☐ PLAYING HOOKY #20 ....15606/$2.75
☐ LEFT BEHIND #21 ....15609/$2.75
☐ OUT OF PLACE #22 ....15628/$2.75
☐ CLAIM TO FAME #23 ....15624/$2.75
☐ JUMPING TO CONCLUSIONS #24 ....15635/$2.75
☐ STANDING OUT #25 ....15653/$2.75
☐ TAKING CHARGE #26 ....15669/$2.75
☐ TEAM WORK #27 ....15681/$2.75
☐ APRIL FOOL #28 ....15688/$2.75
☐ JESSICA AND THE BRAT ATTACK #29 ....15695/$2.75
☐ PRINCESS ELIZABETH #30 ....15715/$2.75
☐ JESSICA'S BAD IDEA #31 ....15727/$2.75
☐ JESSICA ON STAGE #32 ....15747/$2.75

Buy them at your local bookstore or use this handy page for ordering:

Bantam Books, Dept. SVT3, 414 East Golf Road, Des Plaines, IL 60016

Please send me the items I have checked above. I am enclosing $_____
(please add $2.00 to cover postage and handling). Send check or money
order, no cash or C.O.D.s please.

Mr/Ms _____

Address _____

City/State _____ Zip _____

Please allow four to six weeks for delivery.   SVT3-9/89
Prices and availability subject to change without notice.

YOUR OWN

SLAM BOOK!

If you've read *Slambook Fever*, Sweet Valley High #48, you know that slam books are the rage at Sweet Valley High. Now *you* can have a slam book of your own! Make up your own categories, such as "Biggest Jock" or "Best Looking," and have your friends fill in the rest! There's a four-page calendar, horoscopes and questions most asked by Sweet Valley readers with answers from Elizabeth and Jessica.

It's a must for SWEET VALLEY fans!

☐ 05496 FRANCINE PASCAL'S SWEET
   VALLEY HIGH SLAM BOOK
   Laurie Pascal Wenk $3.95